POET & VAMPIRE

POET & VAMPIRE

Chuck Taylor

MadCityPublications
New York, New York
"The only ones for me are the mad ones."

The author wishes to thank the numerous magazines, such as the _Barcelona Review_ online, that published earlier versions of these fictions, poems, prose poems, and bastard mixtures. Unfortunately, the author is in the process of moving, and bibliographic information is packed away in a box.

Cover Art: Chuck Taylor
Book Design: ABP

For orders and information:

MadCityPublications
New York, New York
Madsitypublishers@gmail.com

This book owes so much to so many. I'd like to thank my wife Takako, my children, my many wonderful students who have stayed in touch, and my close artistic compadres Ken Fontenot, Mick White, Chris Carmona, Corina Carmona, Connie Williams, Miguel Juarez, Jerry Craven, and Hedwig Gorski. In my heart are many who have passed, such as David Yates, Raul Salinas, and Ricardo Sanchez.

The best reward of the literary life is the friendships you build.

A special thanks goes out to my twenty-year friend and multi-linguist David Chroust, who is both Czech and American. We get each other's humor and always make each other laugh.

"Would you tell me, please, which way I ought to go from here?"

"That depends a good deal on where you want to get to," said the Cat.

"I don't much care where—" said Alice.

"Then it doesn't matter which way you go," said the Cat.

"—so long as I get SOMEWHERE," Alice added as an explanation.

"Oh, you're sure to do that," said the Cat, "if you only walk long enough."

—Lewis Carroll

When will the younger brothers finally wake up? The wise old ones say it will only happen when the violence in nature is on top of them. And yet what can we do, mere singers, but to keep on singing?

—Author Unknown

CONTENTS

Part Two: "Middle"

Part Three: "End"

POET & VAMPIRE

Part One: "Beginning"

On the Way to San Miguel

Small mud houses Vampire saw when he looked down in the valley, and then he saw the winding paths the people walked to climb barefoot up the steep side of the mountain to the rushing highway, where they spread old worn cloth across dried bushes for protection against the beating sun.

When Vampire came down the road in the screaming burst of metal, like an armed conquistador, these small people, men and women, would hold lizards by the tail, two feet long they'd killed, up for you to purchase and eat.

Vampire never saw one car stop. He wondered how such a large lizard might taste, if cooked over an open fire. He'd stopped once when younger and braver, buying a necklace made of seedpods linked by wire. Vampire wore it off and on till it got lost in a move.

It was hard to stop because Vampire felt like what most feel in the Western world—like rich assholes. He was pleased the Indians stood there though—just sorry they'd had to turn to begging. Vampire knew that they lived a way close to where most the people came from—a harsher life for sure, the hunting and gathering, but home. He knew he still, in part, belonged.

Onion

I am not Borges, Mr. Borges of Argentina wrote, speaking of his writer's self as different from his self-self, but the writer's self of Borges remains the only Borges Poet knows, muses Poet on this page, losing who he is, it seems, making his writer self.

A page is a map of course, but the self in the body's house is no more the I of me than the self on the page. The self's mostly electrochemical flashes down and around the nervous system, brain to heart to toe. You're getting a writer self on the page based on the wiring in this human house.

This wiring has touched at times, even with its limited powers, shadows of other features of a greater house. For one, Poet hopes he says with humility, there may have been flashes of the divine. Poet doesn't like the word God. It makes an ugly ring that sends him back to the fighting times of warrior kings, but the word remains the common one of his time.

This wiring in the house, it knows that bad things have been done. The wiring senses the house has hated mostly groups, rarely simple people in the flesh, and one time, in a dream, the house felt visited by a malevolent form

Poet chased away by repeating over and over the word "Love," but as to what dwells inside the house, the wiring has in all its years never found demon forms, and as a consequence, the wiring wires to the page for the writing self to record, that the wiring self and writing self are not the all that is. The wiring senses shadows and knows it lives in suffering while living in the house that is the body that goes beyond the body, while loving in joy the intricate beauties of the globe and globes beyond, and for all its pessimism, remains an optimist.

The onion waiting in the dark ground, why not call all this in its potentiality for life and for the page that lives in the world, as it waits for the planting of myriad other plants and seeds?

Vampire at Dawn

Vampire returned from his night feeding – as all bats must do at dawn. His insects were larger than what most bats liked, and they were often a greater challenge to catch, but then, humans were violent toward each other and a risk to the planet as a whole, so he felt his nights' work worthy.

Ah humans, busy-buzzing, climate-warming, carbon monoxide creatures, but he liked them anyway, for their beauty and cleverness. Still, he wished more large vampire bats like himself out and about in the world, in order to save the planet of its human mistake and rescue the overheated earth from death by technological plague and unfreezing methane.

But he did not dwell on dark thoughts for long. Vampire loved to watch the sun come up and move across the land, first touching the top leaves of trees, and then working its way down, changing the very nature of reality itself, he thought, making the world something else, more beautiful with its colors, yes, and no doubt more dangerous for those who are seen by devouring eyes. "The rosy fingers of dawn." He did not know where he had learned that phrase.

Mornings made him happy. His belly was full, and soon he would be asleep in his crowded coffin like a happy baby. The light moved so fast! It seemed to reach into almost every corner, and with the light came the warmth. The breezes picked up and things began to stir. He sometimes yearned to be some other kind of creature, a poet of the light perhaps, to write an epic on the coming of the light and its rise in the sky to midday.

With such a story he could fill a thousand pages, using his radar, his sense of sight, and smell. He would not focus on humankind. That had been done. Too many small creatures remained without praise or story, like the grubs and lizards.

If only he had gone to school and learned to write. Still, he realized he had no unique perceptions on the world. He was an earthy creature, sadly without genius.

Optimistic and Positive

"I tell ya'," says Vampire to Poet, "the money's always been on optimism in this country. Look at your Broadway musicals where they're constantly dreaming the impossible dream. That sure ain't Greek tragedy.

And would you look at me? Vampire continues. I'm more optimistic American that you are, even though I'm from old Europe. I fly around, I befriend and rescue pigs, I'm seven hundred years old and in good health. I'm no work or rent slave. Yes, I live a merry-go-round."

"Not that I'm accusing you of anything," says Poet, "but some might call you a serial killer."

"If vampires were human beings, there might be a basis for such a case, but nature's law for my species is different from yours. I must hunt like the gorgeous Black Panther, and require fresh blood to survive. I am higher up on the food chain than you are, and am doing my part, as are other vampires struggle to do around to world, to cull the human herd, to help prevent the total swamping of the globe."

"And so this is thinking optimistic."

"Optimistic and positive. The two are close. The money's definitely in thinking positive and optimistic—two peas in one pod. You've got to believe in what you do. You've got to enjoy your work and feel you are making a contribution. I learned that from your country, and I'm grateful. I sing as I fly through the long and often cold nights, hoping to get lucky and spot a meal. It's important to keep on the sunny side."

Jokes

How many vampires does it take to change a light bulb?

Poet found himself philosophically aroused by this question. He'd watched moths, hundreds of them, at convenience stores, circle obsessively around bright parking lot lights, but bats, they travelled at night and avoided light altogether.

It might require many bulbs, because the chances were the bats would bat a bunch of light bulbs around and break a batch, Poet smiled.

Poet thought if he could come up with a good joke about vampires he could get people to relax and they would not be so scared, but jokes usually were not the province of poets. They should be, thought Poet. We need more jokes in poems. Good belly laughs could be excellent suicide prevention for the dark kind of poet and audience.

How about, how many vampires does it take to sit on the head of a pin and seduce a virgin? Poet had read somewhere that lions will not eat a virgin. Talking about Eros, however, seems unpopular these days. You could bring in all the zombies you want. Heads and arms are allowed to drop off in the streets. The stink of death can be horrendous everywhere. Men with rockets and machine guns can mow down people in the movies right and left—live people, not zombies—and nobody seemed to mind.

But Eros—something that could bring pleasure and life instead of pain and death—that subject was dangerous. Poet had to admit he himself was squeamish. He didn't like the idea of cross-species coupling, mating between humans and vampires, as was suggested these days in some genre novels. That struck him as bestiality, rather disgusting.

What would you get if you cross a vampire and a viper. How about a vipvamp? Or cross a vampire and an orca whale?

Dumb idea, Poet decided

How about: So this vampire walked into a bar . . .

Oh, I know what you want, the owner says. You'd like a Bloody Mary. Let me get you a bartender. Hey Mary, there's a gentleman here to see you.

Chuck Taylor

Generational Stress

"You're going to get an education and become a brain surgeon, got that kid?"

That's what Poet's uncle down the street said to him, Miller Beer in hand, watching the White Sox on TV, black and white in 1957. His pants buckle was undone and his belly fat rolled forward like it was about to do a mudslide down his legs.

"Yeah, a brain surgeon, and then you can operate on your aunt and get her wires uncrossed."

"Ah come on Uncle Charley, you know what I'm going to do," Poet said. "I'm going to be a white water rafting guide through the Grand Canyon, and when I get too old for that I'm headed for Paris to teach English."

"And leave your family behind, who feeds you and gives you a place to sleep?"

"Well, I do cut lawns. I make my own money."

"Yeah, and one of them is mine. Before you do the cutting, take a look in the backyard."

"I'm kind of rushed. Can you tell me?"

"You'll see it when you cut. I built you a pen, and it's got some strays I picked up on my milk route that last few weeks in the mornings."

"Strays?"

"Yeah, for brain surgery. You do a science project and you'll win a scholarship to college. Your cousin Mary can help. She wants to be a nurse. You're that smart, kid. I believe in you."

Chuck Taylor

What Men Don't Usually Do

Carrying a gun he came, the unknown neighbor, through the hollyhock dividing their yards, a man with hidden eyes who rang the backdoor bell Saturday morning, "The pigeons," he said, "I'll kill the birds for you in your eaves."

Poet was eating his eggs sunny side up when he heard the man speak on the steps. Poet's body began to shake. Why kill the pigeons whose cooing he found comfortable in the morning? The birds were family, lovely to know and be with.

Poet studied the pigeons high on their house. He saw them at the stops on the elevated train he rode with his mother to downtown Chicago when she shopped at Fields. The pigeons, they moved in a kind of dance in all kinds of colors.

Poet at four was a quiet child. He suffered from asthma and wondering at times if his breath would fail in the middle of the night. He already sensed the world was cruel, but why add to the misery?

So in his fear he found a voice. He pleaded with his dad across the breakfast table, as he'd never done before, to spare the birds. His father looked in his eyes and read his agony, and sent the man away. He did a thing that men back then didn't usually do.

Befriending Alligators

As yet, no one has made the effort to befriend an alligator, Vampire observes. He is a bit disappointed. Humans have such an all-consuming desire to be hugged, cuddled, and loved, and in the process of being loved, to imperialize and eliminate every kind of other — that which is alienate and different — to make one big, happy, Jesus universe of family. We're all actually alike, right?

Perhaps it comes from guilt at having decimated so many species, like the buffalo, and having eliminated others entirely, like the carrier pigeon, Vampire observes.

Humans have befriended Vampires, yes; Saint Frances befriended his birds; Disney had his mouse. Lions have been befriended as cubs and later set free in South Africa, only to recognize their former human friends. Dolphins have been befriended and put to work making money for their Sea World keepers. Elephants are tamed like horses and cattle and make their economic contributions. In Vietnam, inside dogs are pets. Outside does are eaten. Orca whales, the Free Willy types, have both befriended their keepers and killed them. South African farmer Marius Els raised and befriended Humphrey the Hippo as an orphan child, and came to see him as his own son, with unfortunate results, and by that Vampire means the hippo gorged him to death and left him floating in the water.

And then there is Timothy Treadwell, the Grizzly Man. Treadwell gets all the credit in the thirteen years he spent documenting on film his relationships with bears. His girlfriend, Amie Huguenard, did most the filming and only once or twice does one catch a glimpse of her on camera. Ever faithful to her filmmaker's job, she got eaten right after filming Timothy being finished off.

Vampire suggests humans don flippers, masks, and green wet suits with bumps like the monster in the movie, *Creature from the Black Lagoon,* so the alligators will feel as if the humans are similar, even if alligators can smell the difference. Humans can bring gifts of food, say a dead chimp or baby lamb, as offerings. Feeding the alligators, as you swim amongst them, petting and giving hugs, will seem like feeding pigeons in the park. Why sure, some alligators may feel they're not getting their fair share of lamb or chimp, and in a fit of hungry pique, bite through some humans, but why worry? So many humans out there are dying from wars, car wrecks, self-inflicted gunshot wounds, and school shootings, but still plenty remain. Just think how the science of alligators will be advanced.

You can't blame the alligators, says Vampire. We all have to eat. Humans don't know what it's like not to have grocery stories, and no food banks exist, along the banks of rivers, to assist any sad, desperate alligator.

Chuck Taylor

Dreams Do Come

A beast holds Poet upside down with a hand so large the creature can wrap his fingers around Poet's two ankles. The beast is eyeballing Poet, and with a heavy machine manipulated carefully, removing, with tiny tweezers, all of Poet's eyelashes.

When the beast is done he'll return Poet to his metal cage at Plato 666, in the metal barn of steel cages where poets are stacked one on top of another. The poets can get their heads through their cages' bars, and eat from a conveyor belt carrying scraps of meat and vegetables sweeping slowly before them. What they don't eat comes circling around again.

The beasts do the eyelash plucking every six months, when the poets' lashes have grown fully back. Still, Poet is as scared as a child petrified by an imaginary monster under the bed. Poet doesn't know for sure what his eyelashes get used for, but he suspects they get crushed into oil that's needed for the miniature gears in Nano robots. Lashes are too small for stuffing—the elder down that's plucked from living geese to put inside pillows. The beasts are convinced that the eyelashes of poets make the finest oil, due to poet sensitivity.

Poet's worried because he does not know how long, with all the plucking, his lids will hold together to create more lashes. If they fail Poet could get chopped up and cooked up like chicken fried steak—or killed and tossed into the trash, to be buried underground to ferment into agricultural fertilizer.

On the other hand, it's been a long time since Poet has felt this important.

Enjoy, if You Can

Poet, who is, after all, a lowly worker of words, considered superfluous by his time, a person who lives by solitude, who studies the soft breezes of the mind and heart, well, this forgotten Poet being written about here, has been surprised to discover on a couple of occasions that women, a few, were pretending to love his poetry, but what they really wanted was to make it with him. He's not here to brag. It didn't happen but twice.

Poet was flattered that anyone could care that way for him, not being what he considered blessed by movie star looks, and a bit disappointed that his poems did not actually have someone who loved them, but Poet knows how it goes with smart women who are capable of reading poetry. They're not dysfunctional and the making it would be expected to lead to more—some of that, more making it in bed—but more of it, Bed and Bath stuff, carpets and curtains and chairs and comforters and houses and mortgages and jobs, plus children, in 99% of the cases, but Poet has already tried that, and it didn't go perfectly. The work to keep that train running on time stressed him out and made him turn at times suicidal—and kept him a million miles from his pen.

So why do it all over again? Poet's a quiet man, a misogynist to boot, and no rollicking rock star.

Please just read and enjoy, if you can.

Vampire Discovers

Vampire peers in more and more windows to view lovely women stretched out asleep, their necks glowing in the milky bright moonlight, but more often than not the women's windows are shut and locked, and the women sleep more and more alone. The vampire in his travels has seen it spreading, and a woman sleeping alone does make his job easier. The idea arrived in the industrial nations first—the notion that it was time for humans to stop engaging in coupling.

Pornography had made humans fearful that they did not look beautiful enough and that they did not know how to engage in the erotic passionately. It wasn't passion humans were seeing actually, with actors acting like machines, but the many humans did not seem to know that. Hoards of sexually transmitted diseases had popped up everywhere in laboratories on slides viewed through powerful microscopes, and the homes for what were mostly viruses were expected to be the human sexual organs. Vampire can't say their names of these organs because the NSA could be trolling them as keywords in their search for evil people. "Evil people" is a euphemism for another word Vampire can't say for fear of the Patriot Act. Vampire wants all listeners to know, though born overseas, he is a PATRIOT!

But anyway, parents in the old days had begotten children, and put up with them through the useless early years, so they could get free labor later on farms, and then they'd be around to take care of their parents in old age and inherit the farm. A certain nostalgia for children hung on in the air, especially among women, well into the urban age, but now children have grown too expensive to educate through college, only to see them leave for faraway places at twenty-one to work in retail.

Men knew of their women's nostalgia and felt they could not be trusted, so they beat off more and more in the shower, or got vasectomies before marriage. There were too many humans anyway and less and less room for other animals. The polar ice caps were melting. Food had skyrocketed upwards in price with global climate change, and what a couple could manage to grow in their small suburban yards could not even feed two dogs.

Vampire does not know how long the death of Eros will last, but more women sleeping alone are available to feed on if he carries with him a good glasscutter and tape to quietly remove the window blocking him. As he works, Vampire imagines how the loss of Eros must be painful to humans. He imagines their bodies must hunger for Eros as he hungers for blood.

Chuck Taylor

Pigs

What do I know about pigs? You might ask, said Vampire. Well, I am not always in immediate need of blood—and thus chasing humans. My first acquaintance with pigs was on a family farm in Kansas, where the pigs kept chasing me wanting to sniff and playfully nip at my leather shoes.

Perhaps they picked up on some wonderful smell left over from the curing of the leather, which neither humans nor vampires are able to pick up. Pigs' noses are much longer and thicker, like dogs, much superior at detecting odors. I had to laugh at the situation, a pack of pigs after a vampire just beginning to experience the rumblings of hunger in his belly.

Farms are generally far from the law and from prying eyes—good places for vampires to operate. Well, I didn't get any supper that night, but I did begin my long love affair with those smart and social animals we have misnamed pigs.

I knew a pig once that lived on a lovely beach in Mexico. I have a photograph of him singing to the full moon, something he did often. Pigs are stuffed in small pens and left to defecate on themselves. A pig's skin is highly sensitive and often lacks shade. They are forced to cover themselves in mud to protect their pink skin from horrible sunburn.

Whenever I'm working a farm, after I've supped, I will always set pigs free from their pens. I can see in their eyes gratefulness, and love to watch them move into the fields under the wide stars, noses to the ground.

Chuck Taylor

Poet in the Autopsy Room, Trying to Train to be a Surgeon

I've been with the dead, the many dead,
as they lay naked on stainless steel tables,

prepared for the final ritual, an intimate
conversation, without words, with a group

of the living. I have studied the dead's faces.
Their mouths, their open eyes, their eyebrows—

those parts especially but also their faces as
a whole, looking for an answer, any answer,

some explanation, but the faces of course
remain still. They don't express surprise,

pain, regret—no, just a blankness. I admire
the courage of these dead who have been

waiting patiently in their hospital rooms.
They are never embarrassed to be naked.

They don't mind that we slice them open
to weigh their organs. They speak to you

through their smell, come right up inside
your nostrils, and I, superstitions since I am

alive, always say a few words as prayer as
the dead get rolled back inside their cool

boxes. I'm never here when the men in black
hearses, the undertakers, come to take them

to the funeral homes, to their caskets, to
the service at the church or in the funeral

home, and then outside, for the ride to
the cemetery, where, at last, the undertakers

take their bodies and put them safely under
the soil, silent, unsurprised at their coming.

Chuck Taylor

Forget GI Joe

Says the ant-papist Vampire, never a friend of crosses, I want to be a Pope wearing a tall hat and glorious sweeping robes, but not just any Pope, a fighting Pope who leads armies, who carries a sword, who swears oaths and waves his crest and cross to encourage believers to charge up San Juan Hill like Teddy Roosevelt to save the Holy See. No ordinary papacy for me. Slash and burn like General Sherman. No tiny Vatican City. I will have many Papal States, I will have many mistresses, and I will have at least twelve illegitimate children in honor of the apostles. I won't be the first Pope of this kind. There are historical precedents, models for me to emulate. I will deliver, using the best sound systems manufactured for rock bands, magnificent speeches to the faithful in the Vatican square from the Papal balcony. We will bring back Latin, we will bring back censorship, and we will bring back the sixty-hour workweek so people will have less time to sin. No abortions even during our army's times of rape and pillage. No birth control, not even the rhythm method. I will take pleasure in sumptuous feasts of many courses of rare delicacies. Someone has to do it, to show on earth what can be done in the name of God, and to give us a glorious image of heaven. My subjects will live through me. Together we will make the church triumphant.

Grand Theft Auto

Vampire is drawn to the medieval gothic churches with the skeletons in lovely glass cases along exterior stonewalls draped with jewels and thin chains made of gold. Vampire always picks a quiet time in the church, a time when the shadows are thick in the sanctuary.

Will the skeletons miss their gold and gems? Vampire does not think so, and doubts there are surviving relatives who will notice. Vampire has an excellent glasscutter and can't put together a life on blood alone.

Our Vampire needs a new pair of shoes. Pigs nicked up the old ones, plus, during his down time, Vampire likes to waste hours and hours playing video games. He wants the new version of "Grand Theft Auto."

Chuck Taylor

College Education

Poet liked to crawl in the bedroom windows of his students. "You're not keeping your dream journal," he would shriek, startling the student awake. "You got it right next to your bed, like I told you, but the pages are blank. You haven't written down a single dream."

"Listen," said the sleepy student. "I'm paying a lot of money to live in this dump of a dorm even though I don't want to be here. When I leave I need to make more money than I paid while here and I need to make it fast so I can get out of debt and be happy. Don't you see? It's that simple."

"It's not my fault you haven't dreamed up any money making inventions," said Poet. "You could at least dream up a shower curtain with poems printed on it to read while taking your shower, a curtain that keeps the floor perfectly dry, or you could dream a door that spots Jehovah's witnesses and Dravidians, tosses lemon pies in their faces, and tells them to move on, they're trespassing."

"Some professor you are, Poet, picking on God like that," said the student. "If you're so smart, why ain't you rich?"

Droning On

When a drone is swooping down on your house or your car, you have no time to respond. You can't chant verse at a certain frequency that would confound its signal and knock it off track so it stalls and falls on a far off dusty field and does no damage. You can't aim your rifle and shoot it out of the sky.

Poet's afraid these drones are going to get much smaller and more lethal, as well as more impervious to being knocked out of the sky. They're still going to hit the wrong homes and kill the innocents within them. Nothing works 100% all the time. Local police are buying them right now. A time may come when they replace the red light cameras cities have that photograph your license plate and mail you a ticket. Instead, a drone will come and blow up your car, probably with you inside.

Suppose you're shopping at the mall, and you accidentally pick up a pair of socks and put them in your pocket and forget to pay. When you get back to your car and turn on the ignition, the drone will know where you are and fall on you, once you're away from other cars.

With drones patrolling the sky night and day, they'll be

able to hit the drug dealers and their customers as soon as they dealers hand over the drugs. Soon America will be as safe a place to live as Singapore.

"What's the problem?" many ask. "They're already tracking your calls. They easily and always know where you are since you carry a cell phone. You and Vampire, you're good guys and got nothing to worry about, right?"

Poet's Afraid

You're out at dusk in the woods,
the rain starts slashing down,
the lightning starts forking from
the winter sky into leafless trees.
Should you find something tall

for your safety, say a sycamore
along a creek? Or lie in the grass
flat in a low part of an open field?
It's love. It's love, always love, no
matter what the situation. You car

is an hour's walk away. You saw
dark clouds to the east an hour
ago. You knew what was coming.
Stay calm, it's the world, not her,
you love. Storms eventually pass.

Chuck Taylor

Meet Meat

Where's the meat and what's the beef? Nietzsche should have said that. Poet recalls being in a glass bottom boat, young and hungry, staring down at a coral reef, wondering if anything down there could be considered meat and might make a nifty treat.

Take a seat. The meat of it is the meat of it. The heart of it is the heart of it, and it too is pure pumping meat. Nietzsche should have said that. Cut to the chase, those stupid English dogs ballyhooing those terrified foxes. Eventually the master gets the meat on his plate up at the Manor. Machiavelli could have said that.

Poet's been in those cold warehouses with the hanging hooks of cow caucuses. They're infinite. Rocky Balboa got to punch them. There's something like the flag in all-American meat, wouldn't you say? It belongs on the fifty-yard line. The red. The blood. The dead.

Many hold that meat can move you, as the earth moves in a fracking earthquake, when properly prepared. Meat belongs to the Marines, and gives them strength and mobility. Yes, meat looms like beer. You can't claim to be a man unless you take to it like a pickup truck.

Paradise is a good day's barbeque in the backyard.

Psst. Hey you, don't you love to pull open a can of sardines, and see those silver angels laid out precise, like the insides of old transistor radios? It's not as good as beating the meat of Eros, working that old sausage, but damn close, birddog, damn close.

Cow, Philosopher, Poet

Poet's Welsh Black rambled to his back door this morning. She'd had six black calves, and now behind her was a white. You could read the question in her eyes, "This… can't…be?"

A cow is like a woman. No woman should view this statement as an insult. Most who say it are being mean and stupid. Poet's never seen a fat cow on his farm or on any of his neighbors. You don't get fat munching grass. For nine months cows like human women carry their babies, and they nurse after birth from nine to twelve months. Poet's former spouse actually nursed for two years.

Cows will take turns babysitting each other's calves. One will be at one end of a field with the calves while the other moms are busy grazing. When she feels she's put in her time and is beginning to be taken advantage of, she will call till another cow comes, or walk toward the center of the field.

Troubled by a busy schedule? Calm yourself by standing under a blue cloudless sky with cows. Stare into their deep brown eyes. You will find meanings no philosopher knows because he's too busy proving HE, and no other creature, human or animal, can be right.

Poet sees more of god in a cow than in any poet or philosopher he has yet to meet, in part perhaps because no cow desires to be a god. He still hopes for a single poet, or philosopher, as noble and wise as a cow chewing her cud, swatting the flies away with her tail, skillfully, calmly.

Like the NSA, Poet's Always Listening

Orgasms, from across the coffee
shop Poet hears the young salesman
talking about his lover's orgasms
on an old cell phone — to another guy,
it's obvious. Who'd dare speak
of orgasms to a sister or mother?
The man's words ring enthusiastic.
He speaks no put-down four-letter
words and does no rough masculine
bragging. No love slides in his tone
of words, but from where Poet sits
he can see a glow around the man's
body — or is that the window behind
him? Poet swears he can almost make
out the colorful wide-spread plumage
of a bird-of-paradise. The man says
he's leaving this evening by plane for
Detroit and can't wait till he gets back
and they can be in bed to make flying
up and up organisms The man laughs
into his phone, just before he spots
Poet listening. He frowns, now upset,
a bit embarrassed, and stands up to
meet the hard and chilly rain outside,
quiet, slapping shut his old cell phone.

Inspiring Poem

Poet's certain as rain he's never, in his long life, sat down to write a poem that was inspiring. Nothing wrong with coal dark poems that take you down inside the mine, but nothing wrong, either, with poems that fly up into the golden sunshine.

Some folks think that's the only job for poetry—to inspire—and they want swarms of inspiring poems flying around like locusts, but Poet's not going to let himself get backed into any corner. Still, yes, right now, in this moment, he'll try to write an inspirational poem.

He'll begin by telling you his high school baseball team racked up a five and four season—one more win than loss—but then the team went on to take the state of Illinois baseball championship in the highest class, triple A he thinks it was.

They were called a Cinderella team, but they did it all without a fairy godmother. Today, tomorrow, or next month, you might go from five and four season to a state championship. It's historical. It can actually happen.

Dig for those diamonds in the coal dark of your soul and haul them up. As you work, notice the golden light out of your fingertips. So many you's in you that one or more, at least, was meant for miracles.

Can you recall the kind acts done by strangers? A hand reached out, as you stood on the curb of a busy street, and grabbed you by the collar, to keep you from stepping in front of a bus. Ah, all the anonymous love that has reached for you and saved!

Have you counted the resurrections of the day? A man or woman has turned a crank to flood a field to grow rice to feed you. Everywhere you look the eye meets something hungering for attention. Poet's in love with the metal coil of spring that clipboards down this poem.

Overpopulation

I know I'm not the only one checking text messages and emails on my cell phone, says Vampire, at this very moment in this lapidary town, but I could be the only one with a ladybug that's landed on my left shirt sleeve, I could be the only one wondering what my friend, the steel booted Putin, ate for breakfast in Moscow May 16th, or was he at his dacha? I hope the weather was pleasant and lifted the leader's mood toward former territories that have left the Russian fold.

I could be the only one that hears the herd of elephants on the moon's dark side, what with my super Vampire hearing. They are playing on a wind-up RCA Victrola Coltrane's "Love Supreme."

I wish to be the only one, I want to be that special on this crowded globe, and I want to be blessed by a solitude that needs mixed in the pain of loneliness, so to feel the horrid rush of time as these humans seem to need to feel, like the wind whooshing by in their ears. I wonder if there's anyone out there now, in this lapidary town, rolling pill bugs in the dust like a child?

Desire

An overwhelming desire to kill—yes, Poet did know someone like that. Actually, Poet has brushed against several like that, but only one closely. He was then Poet's brother-in-law, a Vietnam veteran, and he could sit all the long day in a chair at Poet's house, drinking one beer after another, staring at the wall.

Edward wasn't thoroughly bad. He helped his sister (then Poet's wife)—yes, he helped them move their belongings from El Paso to Salt Lake City with his pickup truck. Still, Edward often heard voices and had been diagnosed by the VA as a paranoid schizophrenic.

Edward had always felt less than a man since a superior officer ordered him to kill some Viet Cong prisoners, and found he could not do it.

Edward would tell Courtney, "I could kill you." He would say the same to Poet. When he said it, Poet said nothing back. Courtney always replied, "Yes, I know, Edward."

A part of Edward was incomplete and he would suffer miserably the rest of his days, until he had accomplished what needed to be done to make himself whole. Indeed, Edward shot and killed a man in the back of the head at a biker party in Edmund, Oklahoma, in front of about fifteen people.

No one would show up in court to testify against Edward. The word was put out through the biker community that you'd be killed if you did show up. Twice the district attorney tried to put Edward in prison, but the case was finally dismissed for lack of evidence.

Edward, Poet last heard, had moved in California, and was doing time for a drug-related crime. He had gotten pregnant a retarded woman. Courtney travelled from Utah to California and tried to claim the child to raise herself, but the court judged her to be too poor.

Edward, Poet wants you to know he prays and hopes that you are indeed finally whole, or as close to whole as humans get.

Crow

Vampire has been living his life with a crow on his shoulder that he calls Tommy so people will feel comfortable around him. Tommy is his third crow. Before him Vampire boarded Crow Joe on the shoulder and before that Jim Crow.

The bond he's felt with these beautiful and brilliant creatures remains indescribable. The world is learning how sweet and amazing they are. All his crows have whispered prophecies in his ear, such as "Don't eat the third from the top rolling hot dog at the convenience store because the meat is bad and will make you sick, and besides, it's totally bloodless". Or, "Your car battery will go dead in the movie theatre parking lot two weeks from today."

Vampire's crows—all three—somehow could sense who was about to give him trouble. Their "crow eye" looks as disconcerting to humans as the evil eye in many cultures. The only thing Vampire wishes to know is why his crows abandoned their own tribes to shoulder with him. Such a generous act deeply touches his heart and makes him feel a guilty love. The crows rarely slip off his shoulder and fly away, usually only to hunt or to defecate. Vampire feeds them saltine crackers from a pocket whenever the bird touches his ear with a beak, and keeps a bowl of water on the stone floor close to his casket bed.

What can Vampire say? He's a lucky creature. His crow is often a conversation starter with women he passes on the street.

Glowed in the Trees at Sunrise

Vampire says he hasn't always been an itinerant, trolling through the family farms of back alley states like Nebraska and Kansas. No, Vampire was king two hundred years ago, during a high point in the European aristocracy. KING of the CROWS he was—not one loner sitting on the shoulder but hundreds of bright-eyed and shining crows at his feet, always craftier than humans. Vampire sent them out at night in all four directions searching for prey. Of course they could stop and feed along the way.

When they returned at dawn they bowed and cawed "Your Majesty" as best a crow can. The crows chose redheads—real ones. They'd check the eyebrows close to the roots to see if the red was fake and dyed. They'd guide him to the windowsills of sleeping redheads on the next night. Redheads are rare, but amazingly they always found him at least one since they could cover hundreds of square miles.

Bats never appealed to Vampire as companions. They dropped too much guano on the ground. Rats and cats multiplied like rabbits and lacked the gift of flight. They left their pungent urine smell around like a sour smiles wherever they lived. But crows! They were easy to please.

"Snip, snip." He presented each crow with locks of red hair as a token of his royal appreciation, which they wove into their nests so they glowed in the trees at sunrise.

X-Rated

Prose poems, so empty of Eros, observes Vampire. Not that I know much about the erotic—at least between humans. But it's important, since we are a minority species, that we keep our secrets, such as how we mate, or does the male vampire have a peter, or does the female have a baby oven. It could be we mate through our fingers, or our noses. Maybe we're marsupial. Nature has great imagination in this area.

OK, so you don't want Eros visiting your prose poems. How about putting hair on their arms and legs? Where are their belches, farts, and underarm sweat? Do they ever get swept up by a raging muddy river, yet somehow manage to grab a branch and pull themselves ashore? Where's the adventure, the bombs going off, the houses on fire, the Teddy Roosevelts firing guns and charging up San Juan Hill? Where are the pigs screaming to escape the chutes that lead inside the slaughterhouses?

Vampire used to keep some ducks. He built a pond for them but the water was always seeping out, so he stole a children's blue plastic wading pool from the parking lot at Wally Mart. Vampire would exclaim to whatever creatures were around, "Beautiful, aren't they? Masters of water and sky, and not so bad on the ground—they combine the comical and sublime!"

"You know, ducks are considered monogamous birds," Vampire would sometimes lie to human women, to watch them sigh and smile and grow soft-eyed just before he bit them.

Vampire didn't explain how the male ducks grab the females by the neck with their beaks, push their heads to the ground, and then mount from behind, still pressing down the female's head. Their mating is almost over before you notice it. The male gets off and the female waddles on, maybe momentarily flustered or pleased, but soon in full composure.

Vampire's ducks were fairly tame and never shy about doing their rough act in front of others whenever the male got the urge to initiate coupling. Vampire thought of taking his ducks to a biology class when they discussed the birds and bees. Part of the topic would then be covered. Kids would get to see how an avian species at least equal to their own striding kind deal with the issue.

Chuck Taylor

Looking for Work

Vampire, I've mentioned before, needed the shiny coin of the American realm to survive. Times would come when he'd need a new suit or pair of shoes, and so to supplement he'd try out for movies with open auditions that required vampire characters. Vampire could sing with a deep baritone, and dance the old soft shoe, so he always thought that he, the real thing, would be a shoe-in, but things didn't necessarily go that way.

If casting director didn't look pleased during the audition Vampire would throw the old evil eye to scare him into giving him the part.

"Your face is too pasty, your hair's too plastered down, and I'm sorry, you're zero scary," casting directors sometimes said, trying to shake off the evil eye. "Let me tell you, it takes more than Halloween plastic fangs to play a vampire, and why that crow on your shoulder?"

"Get off my stage! I've got a grizzly old coot here that understands the soul of vampire. Just looking at him frightens my socks off. We won't be calling you."

Pussy Idiots

They needed someone to jump out of cake at a birthday party, so Vampire volunteered to play the fool for two hundred bucks.

The party was for a high school Goth girl, and only her Goth friends were invited. Vampire preferred blonds or redheads actually. He got enough of black flying around at night. He'd heard the boyfriends and girlfriends would drink each other's blood, as a kind of love ritual, and that disgusted him. Blood was serious, necessary for survival, and shouldn't be wasted playing silly romantic games.

The cake was a huge round cardboard box with thin paper on top. The box was made in Indonesia, as part of their campaign to cut down their rainforests, and a local confectioner put on the frosting. Vampire had thought of immigrating to Indonesia, but few true blonds or redheads could be found amongst its people. The fake cake was smeared with thin frosting so the top didn't collapse. Vampire brought a small flashlight so he could read Einstein's book on relativity, while he waited inside for his moment to punch out. The Goth girls were all feminists. They didn't want a bikinied chick jumping out of the cake that might run off with one of their boyfriends. No, they wanted something fancifully scary and cool. The birthday girl's best friend was supposed to bang hard on the table with a glass when it was time for Vampire to burst out, but Vampire must have fallen asleep, or maybe he passed out, since vampires like dogs cannot sweat. The imitation cake lacked ventilation and grew suffocating inside.

Finally a Goth girl cracked the lid and shouted, "Wake-up! We paid good money for you to do something scary."

Vampire came out of the cake carefully so as not to get frosting on his cape. He took a few quick steps and then a leap from the table, and flew the circumference of the room twice, cackling loudly every now and then. After that, since he had already been paid, Vampire landed on a windowsill, pulled open the window, and flew out. His audience either ran screaming for the doors where they made a log jam, or tried to climb under the table where the cake sat, yet one girl shouted, "Wait, I want to be your friend. I'll keep you at home in my closet. I'll feed you. My parents will never know. You can drink my hamster's blood."

What a bunch of pussy idiots, Vampire thought, here they are romanticizing death at a birthday party, when they've never seen a person die, or gazed upon a dead body. "I miss my crow," he mumbled.

I Am Here

I wish to be the fairest vampire in the land. Is that too much to ask? Make me movie star handsome—classically cool handsome, smolderingly handsome, bad boy handsome, and pixie boy handsome, a mixture of Cary Grant, Marlon Brando, James Dean, and Brad Pitt.

I am not asking for any flashy beauty, mirror. I won't increase my feeding if you grant my wish to be the fairest in the land, and I promise no hubris, no temper tantrums, no vanity, no poisoned apples, merely a humble pie pride. Are you listening, Magic Mirror? You can see and do anything.

I'm standing right before you in this forgotten castle. Don't you see me? Please, why do you ignore, remain so blank. I am here.

Chuck Taylor

It's All Good, Isn't It?

Vampire needs to remind himself that he is not who his is. None of us are who we are. If we were who we are, we wouldn't spend so much time night and day dreaming. Vampire dreams all the time. Poet dreams all the time. You, reader, dream more than you know.

Do you go around more than once in the subway turnstile? Do you miss your exit on life's highway? Vampire dreams in winter that he's in another planet's spring field of wildflowers. He dreams himself an Olympic tobogganist living in a nudist apartment complex in the musical city of Austin. He dreams baseball games, with the losing Chicago Cubs, up in the high bleachers alone where he won't be bothered.

Vampire lives on many dimensions that are milliseconds apart. His soul is a flashing bulb back and forth six thousand times a second. Vampire is not who he is. Mirror knows this. That's why Mirror is blank. One day Mirror plans to talk to Vampire in Mirror's famous deep and resonating voice.

"There, there," he'll say. "It's all good. Isn't it? You've got your crow."

What Could Be Coming

I hate to be the one to tell, babes in toy land, says Poet, but they're out right there now in their think tank offices, trying to take whatever they can away from you, to take the way you hold hands, to take the rub of kisses across your face, the splay of palms across your naked belly; they're here to make it again a painful duty, a shouted curse, a sin to swallow, formerly a beauty, but now to be endured like stepping on a rusting nail sticking out of a old rotten board half buried in moldering leaves. Yes they're here again and loaded with money and power, already at your ear, to make it dirty again, to degrade the animal sweetness, for it was never to them sacred, and they're lisping, lisping, lisping what they want of you, and you, and you, no escape from suffering or sorrow, never a single hour of grace in fleshly pleasure; they want it a fearful nuclear evil in your bones like strontium ninety, yes you and you and you, you all bear the curse, the blight, the bother. The black of sin lies under your skin, you sinners in the hands of an angry god. Stay therefore in the shadows and drink heavily to keep the black from showing through, daughter of Eve, son of Adam, for she might die young giving birth to your seventh child after she's bourn the painful sin of her duty, but she'll be headed home to heaven, so little need to worry. You'll have a second wife perchance

Chuck Taylor

and without birth control the second will bear four more kids you'll wish all were sons. Too bad you're not on a farm where you can work those kids without a dime of pay, says Poet. Too bad you both must hold down jobs and scrimp in hopes a few might make it to college and come back home to help.

Never Specialize

Poet, to write well, must experience much. That's the way he feels anyway, and you can't talk him out of it. Poet has worked to broaden the narrow suburban view he started his life with. Poet's ridden a stage coach in the 1880's, and a Christmas sled over snow in England with Dickens's friend Tiny Tim, as well as in an ox cart pulled across the virgin plains on the Oregon Trail. He's lived in his car during the depression, and in the woods, by a spring, on a hill, just a few years ago, to get the feeling of closeness to nature known by the author Thoreau. Poet's spent some time in mansions that took up city blocks and in apartments that had rats scurrying in the walls at night keeping the renters awake, but he's never, no never, roomed in a rooming house. He's never sat down night after night in a large living room to be served supper by the landlady and to talk to perfect strangers from all pathways of life. Luckily he has a friend, Daniel, who lives in a rooming house, and sometimes he eats with his friend. The landlady has lots of rules at the rooming house, but that's so everyone can get along and get a good night's sleep. Poet's milked a cow a couple of times, and ridden on hostile horses and cold boxcars. He's walked through the desert with the goat bells tinkling and imagined Jesus at his side, and he's slept on planes and grown evil with seasickness in a storm-tossed boat. He's hiked twenty miles until his feet were screaming, and had a radio show where his butt got tired from sitting. Poet's been lucky. He's even been loved by women and has a couple of kids. Today he's stripping wallpaper off a bathroom wall. Poet wonders, in the paucity of his imagination, after he's hung a new ceiling fan, what wonders yet wait for him to do that might repair the soul?

It Doesn't Get Any Better

Poet became a poet because he believed, in this society, his end would come in his prime, in a flaming crash of Bohemian glory, like a racecar driver, like a soldier fighting in a far off land.

O yes a lonely end, yet an adventurous heroic one, in service of the great flag of art, but when it didn't happen, he changed his mind, quit cigars, and decided to go for the long haul, like Picasso, like Matisse, like Alexander Calder.

Why the rush? He knew where to look for beauty. He'd learned the ways the artist has to transcend the stress to make a meaning. He had his little spider monkey with his tin cup, to stand and recite on corners. Yes! He had seasons and reasons for what he did that he hoped to pass to others.

And so here he is, puffing up Manhattan subway steps, as slow as a bag lady, faceless and average in the swirling mass, not headed for his usual corner, but off to his granddaughter's high school graduation.

Helmet in my Pack

When Vampire finds himself in the great city on a Sunday morning, if he's got spare cash in his pocket, he buys a hundred dollar burgers at McDonald's, then makes his way to Central Park to pass them out to the homeless. Today he's got them hidden in an abandoned baby carriage he found in a narrow alley.

Vampire feels a little like the old ladies who come to feed the pigeons, although Vampire can't sit on a bench and get a flock of homeless to gather at his feet.

"I don't eat that crap," one of the homeless says. "I want organic."

Vampire can't blame them, though he feels one or two-dollar burghers will do more good than harm if you're close to starving. So far the homeless don't try to steal any of his burghers. Maybe out of respect for the baby they think he's carrying.

"Keeping the baby warm with the burgers?" one homeless man asks. "A good idea on a chilly day."

"I don't see you eating this shit,' a shaggy bearded guy says.

"I can't. I'm a vegetarian and don't eat any kind of meat," replies Vampire. "It's a condition I've got," he lies. "My doctor forbids it."

"So you think you're better than us," says a man in dirty blue jogging pants. He comes up fifteen minutes after the last complainer. He takes three burgers. "I am going to report you to the police. You got no health permit."

"I wouldn't do that," says Vampire. "These burghers passed health inspection back where I got them at McDonalds. Besides, you don't want me to sick my crow on you."

"You're some kind of nut?" The man cuts in.

"The crow can do a lot of damage." Vampire rolls his eyes. "There's a bunch of them in the trees of this park, but all it takes is one. All I need to do is whistle. The beak and claws will do the rest."

"Nutcase," the man walks off. "You think I don't have a football helmet in my pack?"

Beauty

All animals have an appreciation for beauty. Ask any male peacock shaking his fan of feathers for the ladies. He knows beauty's magic, how it can be at times unreliable, but at other times pure seductive enchantment. Ask the pig who lives on a Mexican beach and serenades every lonely full moon. Every morning, even in winter, Poet will hear the song of some bird.

Animals find no need to invent zombies or vampires, nor do they write treatises on the gothic or on beauty.

They could philosophize with us on issues of fine art if they wanted to—move beyond waving cat and doggie tails, memorizing parrot lines, or punching chimpanzee buttons—but after dealing with the need for food, they have other things to do, and don't see many of us worth their trouble.

A baby mule deer, if it loses its mother, will search for her on the mountainside for a week, calling and calling, till it grows so weak with hunger it can barely stand. A bear will delicately pull a drowning crow from the water with his teeth, then walk away so the bird can recover from its fright.

Poet can hardly stand it, but it is a beauty, a grieving beauty, a generous beauty.

Vampire and Poet

Arm wrestling, now that might be a civilized way to run a duel between Vampire and Poet, don't you think? No seconds to supervise and hold the pistol cases, no pacing off from back to back, no flintlock firearms.

Which of the great magic arts deserves to be measured superior, that of the fang or that of the tongue?

True, by arm wrestling, one is not setting up a direct duel between fang and tongue, but we want to be of our time and civilized—no serious damage done, this whole book not burned to the ground.

And, anyway, is not Poet a kind of vampire? Is not Poet sneakier in the way he moves around and listens, hiding in plain sight as an ordinary person, sucking out the blood of lives and spitting it off the tongue and onto the page?

And is not the vampire a poet with his subtle appreciation of beauty and with the gorgeous way he brings his—and maybe her—victims to the lovely sleep of death? It is not a death we will come to eventually anyway, in perhaps a less pleasant way?

Vampire and Poet, they sit down at the table opposite from one another. Poet says to Vampire, "Is it not a hollow pumpkin, you dressing up death in your suave art deco aesthetics? I curse you back to your casket, and then I curse your casket into the deepest ice of a mountain Transylvanian winter."

Vampire flashes his fangs and begins to spread his wings. Vampire is a creature of action and dismisses the tongue's flailings from the mouth.

The two stand up and face each other, eyes glaring like sapphires. They forget about arm wrestling.

"Too much seeing has made my blood run bitter," Poet says. "Its river has forgotten the rose. A taste of my neck will kill you."

"I can smell your blood from here," Vampire says. "Your blood would not hurt me, but it would give no delight. Keep your curses where they can do their work. We are not foes. Our magic comes from different springs."

Ekphrastic Poem

This painting, called "The Hospital at Dusk," belongs to no rich collector, nor has ever appeared in a New York show. You won't even find it hanging in some coffee house in Kansas.

Everyone knows the story. How the canvass was done by a vampire, and uses a lot of red. Blood red, that is. Red is good in a painting. It catches the eye. Beautiful women in movies often wear red.

The hospital is an old one, from an old and large American manufacturing city like Lowell, Massachusetts. Its windows, you can tell from the painting, have not been washed in years. The building is about eight stories tall and looks best in the fog of dusk.

Each window in each patient's room, you will notice if you look closely, has an air conditioner window unit hanging out. That's a lot of window units, and the painter, by her use of light and shadow, has kept this repetition from being boring.

People don't like hospitals because these days so many go to die in them, and so the painting is not one many enjoy looking at. There's a rumor, too, that the vampire artist visited the corners of many patient rooms, and gathered antibiotic resistant bacteria. She mixed the bacteria into the paint she used on the painting.

The painting has blood running from the roof, dripping down the sides of the building on the canvass, to remind the viewer how important blood is to the functioning of hospitals.

I, Poet, like the painting because I've a rare blood type that vampires hate the taste of. Years and years ago, before it closed, I made a fair bundle of coin "donating" blood at this very hospital.

Paris Commune

Vampire many years ago found a half-hidden side door in a shadowy alcove. He went up the stairs in a dark narrow passageway, and then pushed open a heavy metal trap door and climbed up on the roof. Where was he? Not in heaven exactly, but on the roof of Sacre Coeur, that sits atop the highest hill in Paris. Most consider the cathedral, consecrated in 1919, an architectural monstrosity, but is it any more ugly than the Eifel Tower? Vampire, a monster himself, knows that Sacre Coeur's monstrosity shouts of its phony moral core, since it was built to expiate the crimes, so-called, of the noble Paris Commune revolt of 1871 that began in its Montmartre neighborhood.

The view from on high, on a cool cloudless morning in June, could have brought the house down in any theatre. Vampire walked the stone stairs and pathways. He admired the heavy stone slabs of the roof. He was at bit flushed with guilt in such a holy secret place, and expected the Old Testament God himself, dressed in a cassock, to jump out of a gargoyle and arrest him. Vampire considered, long and hard, that he might trap pigeons and build little fires to fry them up to sell on the streets, and thus live in this high place, like the Hunchback of Notre Dame, shouting on occasion Proudhon's motto, "Proper-

ty is theft" —until the sorry day he'd be bent by arthritis
and require a carrying down.

Chuck Taylor

It's Almost Perfect

Days come when Poet must be in the mall. Poet knows it's politically incorrect for the literary artist. Not even Vampire will visit the mall. Poet needs the omnipresent tutti-frutti music; he needs the shoppers, as diverse as plants in a forest, in their perceived cool, and the forlorn, blank-gazing salesgirls and boys.

For the moment the shoppers are happy in the hunt, like their hunter-gatherer ancestors, flipping through the racks of clothes with the intense concentration of those who play the Vegas slot machines. The gleaming tile floors, the open skylights full of blue and deathly silent floating clouds, the food court with its crappy burghers and myriad greasy smells, and the giant parking lots surrounding filled with scruffy grackles and glinting beetle cars—all speak loudly of a shallowness that Poet craves and almost loves.

Poet feels the call of nothing in the mall. Oh, maybe he'd like to see a huddle of giant penguins waddle along, or a coterie of prairie dogs barking, or a knot of toads hiding in a corner, but no, Poet just walks and walks, eyes glazed over, in his own delicious mix of meditative alienation.

Bad Fences Make Bad Neighbors

Vampire was not happy with the gusty wind that made flying impossible. It showed up, an unjust gust of a guest at his walk home party. It blew his fancy black hat over a six-foot chain link fence. Being seven hundred, Vampire had to prove his macho by trying to climb over the chain link fence. He made it, puffing away as if he'd just finished a long race, with the grace of a drunken clown.

Unfortunately, Vampire cut his arm on the top sharp edge on the climb back, and had to use his hat to staunch the bleeding. What's a little blood to a hat? Vampire thought. Vampire can get it re-blocked, he's sure, if he searches out a store on the Web. He'll have them leave the blood on, so he can make up lies that tell the truth about the ever-present barbarity.

A Vampire Considers if What She Does is Wrong

So, you know, the pears fall down from the trees in autumn. Unnoticed they darken and grow soft in the grass and nobody bothers to pick them up. They rot on the ground—but we can in no way despair, for we are aware that nothing is lost. Their energy goes back to the earth and flows on into other lives, perhaps grubs or worms or insects.

In the front lawns of America, the American beauty Roses, their comely enflamed petals do wrinkle and fall, to be blown away with the autumn breezes. Death—we all should know—is a part and parcel of life, in no way opposed to life at all, unless we let our egos get in the way. Space needs to be cleared for the coming of the fresh and new.

And, well, let's be honest, more female human babies survive than male babies every year. Something has to be done, and that's where female lesbian vampires come in. They bring the ratio of male to female closer to one to one, so that pernicious practice of polygamy does not return, and God's system of monogamy can be maintained.

I—a mere vampire—am part of the grand scheme of

things, the plan of God, to iron out certain knots through his gloriously intricate web of nature. Wolves, as you know, cull from the herd of caribou the weak and the old. As to male vampires, and why they are here, that's a question I am constantly asking myself. So far, no answers.

Exchange Your Coffin for a Tanning Bed

"All I ask," said the lady to Vampire, "is that you don't take a bite of me until we're married, and that you pledge yourself with a padlock attached to a bridge over the River Seine in the city of lovers, Paris. I'll go with you to make this pledge. When we get to Paris we'll stay in separate rooms."

Vampire was stunned. "But…but, he said, I just came in through your open window."

"And of course I want a big and marvelous wedding, a thousand of my dearest friends and even distant relatives attending, with two live bands playing on separate stages and a seven-foot fountain of champagne—I have a dear friend in the wedding business who can make all the arrangements."

"But we just met. I sleep at night in a wooden coffin with barely room for one."

"I'm a modern post feminist woman, a college graduate with a law degree. Those are my terms. I have the paper for you to sign here in the drawer by my bed."

"What makes you think my kind can read or write, that we have any experience with school at all?" Vampire turned and headed toward the window, whispering under his breath, 'bad blood, bad blood.'

"I could never be with anyone who makes less than a hundred thousand a year," she said. "I bet you don't even have your GED. Besides, you smell too much of cobwebs, and your skin looks as bad as the moon."

IRS

Vampire knows you're not as good as fresh baked bread, and no, you've never done the postal shooting thing ever over at the IRS, though there have been times frustrated workers shredded documents.

Vampire's had friends who've worked in the flat roof sprawl east of I-35 in Austin, and they've joked, over beers—in pure humor only—of flying an airplane over the plant with a large electromagnet to wipe the data free of its servers.

Poof! Gone!

Of course they couldn't afford, or find to hire, such a plane and pilot.

But that's not why Vampire is riled. Let Vampire say here and forever that he is not opposed to paying taxes, even though he's not human and the IRS doesn't make chimps pay taxes. What he's opposed to is the domination of numbers that squeeze the blood out all living creatures, and wants to replace our arteries and veins with the flow of digits through fiber optic cables surgically implanted inside the body's tender blushing flesh. You know the obvious: the planet and its animals are not robots or computers, and cannot be kept alive, in this country or any other that collects taxes, by a digital flow of numbers. If governments continue down such an evil slope, there could be a world revolt.

What Vampire wants to know is why we can't pay our taxes in cords of wood, in nails, in honey, by doing alterations, or by blood.

Vampire at Seven Hundred

We're all supposed to care but I get tired of caring day and night. How about you? Maybe it's because my belly's full. Maybe it's because I'm seven hundred that I don't care if the dishes get done, if the laundry gets folded and put away, if the grass gets mowed, if the roof leaks water on my coffin bed when the rain comes down hard from the north. A century ago I had servants for these domestic problems. Now I change the oil and install a new battery in the car myself. The hot water heater's sprung a leak and the linoleum's coming up from the kitchen floor.

I should call the people I love but I care too little to remember their names. There are blood relatives somewhere. Some may be hungry. Some may have distended bellies—sad, ugly bellies, full of worms perhaps, but I don't care. Aren't we fighting a bunch of wars everywhere? Aren't we always? It's not only our side that's dying but I don't care for either side. Aren't there veterans on our streets, veterans committing suicide, veterans who can't get treatment? I want to care. I should care. But it's too much. The country's too big. It generates too many problems. I need to move back to Europe, maybe Norway. I think I could care in a country of five million. Certainly a manageable number, a reasonable number that leaves plenty of room for trees as well as tragedies.

I'm embarrassed to tell you how much I don't seem to care. It might bother me more if I were human. I guess there's been another school shooting. If I found the energy to care, after another hard day hunting the back roads for blood, what could I do with my tepid emotions? Post something on Facebook? Call up the NRA and file a complaint? The world is too much with us. Getting and spending, we are not recycling our powers. I could tell you who said that, be proper and name the source, but I don't care. I would care to have a good stiff drink but my doctor's said "No go." Doctor's who know how to treat vampires are rare. They're on the old side too.

I'm pruning here in this poem. I'm cutting away the dead branches of the soul, trying to reach some living green where I might deeply care, some bedrock of sorts to start building or budding some lovely flowers of worry, but I don't care if Wendy wins the Texas governorship, I don't care if the Republicans call her abortion Barbie. I don't care if they ever find that Malaysian passenger plane that disappeared at sea. All those crying families on TV, all that pain displayed or not displayed on the news, it could have been staged on a sound studio in Hollywood. Just how much can a vampire take?

What ever happened to that country of rubble they used to call Syria? How are the Egyptians doing under the rule of the military? Who is right, Israel or Palestine, the Navaho nation or the United States? Once inside this dark heart a fire burned like an eternal ruby, but now, well, I'm old, and I have little concern. You'd think I'd care enough to be embarrassed that I don't care. A vampire should hire a PR firm and do some charity work, like Lance Armstrong, to improve the image of the vampire community

—at least, at least, a little caring motivated by self interest, but no, all I can say is please be better than I am. Take care of yourself—don't smoke and don't sleep in old dusty coffins—so when you get old your bones won't ache and you can do some caring.

Vampire Grumpy, Going Marxist, and The NSA Already Knows

I wish, at times, to suck from a capitalist.
I see their stores and feel their iron fists

everywhere, but I can't seem to find them
anywhere. No they're not those sweet little

businessmen in their little vans scrubbing
your carpets or trimming your poodles.

The big guys live on tax-free offshore
islands now, behind walled estates. They

fly to work in private jets. I'd even like to eat
a capitalist. I'd smother with garlic to yummy

the flavor. Of course they're made of nuts
and bolts and hard to chew and swallow

for a guy that works by fang and not by
tooth. Capitalists probably know what

we're thinking years before we're thinking
it. Their advertising agencies are just that

slick. They offer us fat capitalist burghers
and old fat capitalist wine and cigars and if

I should persist, they know now how to
laser zap me from high in outer space, from

a capitalist efficient and Russian built (to
save their dollars) top secret satellite.

Vampire Tries More Poesy

"The trouble with you, Poet, is you don't write poetry," said Vampire. "Poetry takes rhymes and lines. You've got no rhymes or lines. Let me show you how to make a poem. I got seven hundred years of experience behind me, and have been with the dead, so I can do a poem for you on the spot:

> *When I fly out at night in search of blood*
> *I rarely ever find myself stuck in the mud.*
> *I do not feel the need to brood and brood,*
> *Guided by the moody light of heaven's moon.*
>
> *You'll never read it in the German mag* Der Spiegel,
> *But the truth is I fly like a mature Golden Eagle.*
> *In the night I rarely experience any fright*
> *Since I am way too high for hounds to bite.*
>
> *To be a Vampire has been my chosen fate*
> *And what I do is not based on any kind of hate.*
> *I drink the blood of black or white or brown,*
> *Whatever beautiful that happens to be around.*

Poet wanted to dig with his fingers a hole in ground, but he held himself upright by bright smiling and pretending to listen. Our Bard did it out of friendship. This was hard-

Chuck Taylor

ly the first time he'd been so required.

"You're clever at rhyme," Poet replied. "You've even got in some good slant rhymes."

Spells

The days of black do come, just as they come to a Nietzsche worshipping teenager, when Vampire struggles to climb out of his casket. These are of course good days, many—those clichéd sunny days—since the vampire left the old world and moved to the Southern USA.

Ah but these days of black, if Vampire makes it out of the coffin, he can't find the wherewithal to put on his underwear, let alone his black tuxedo and cape, plus his white starched shirts. It's just too wide a river for an old Vampire to swim.

These are days when Vampire's dead mother crosses the ocean to squat on his shoulder like a Poe's raven. You can't go out, she rasps. Nevermore. It's too much. Think of your father. All his years of toiling and what did it get? Why not the recliner? Why not the TV soaps? Forget the blood of life and mix yourself a martini.

Some kind of cobweb has been spun around Vampire's soul. He's trapped in a cocoon, food for baby spiders.

Why was he not born a statue in a lovely side-street Paris park? Why must a vampire do and do?

He would have enjoyed the congregation of birds on his head. Yes, especially crows.

Part Two: "Middle"

Consumptive God

There must be freedom out there. We can't give up. Don't you love the vibrations frothing up out of the ground, enough to make a human sea sick, the rocking and rolling of your morning alarm, the rocking and rolling of your morning drive to work, and how you love the freedom of your rolling office chair, Poet, and how you love the freedom of your six drawer desk. Such a wide world of wordy papers inside!

Go ahead; be free! Stick a chunk of chewing gum under every drawer. God is generous. He said to Poet, you wanted to be born in Peoria, right? No need to lie. I can read your mind. You wanted to fall in love over and over again and again, to be led gently into the rosy garden of the Sonic Drive Inn by the prong between your legs. That's the way I made you guys.

And you liked all the wars too, all the fun on the news, the blood slashing up all the Humvee windshields. You were given time enough to work and spend, right? Up and around the bed and bend, don't need a why, don't need to be shy, just up and buy. Freedom.

Companionship

Vampire had a green-gray slug that liked to sleep in his ears. He was a musical slug, and had a soft buzzing way of humming Beethoven's 5th Symphony. It was relaxing, and helped Vampire—a nervous sort—fall asleep. Vampire had no idea what the slug lived on, besides water, but suspected earwax. During the years they lived together Vampire's ears were clean as a soccer referee's metal whistle, and Vampire could hear much better than usual. Hearing is essential to a creative stalking at night.

During the late afternoons, while Vampire worked off and on various part time jobs, Pierre stayed on a plate with a little water on it, covered by a second plate, back at the house, on the back porch. The slug always looked slightly worried when Vampire left. His lovely small antennae would tremble in the air. Vampire was convinced slugs preferred damp, dark places where they were safe from the dangerous diving beaks of birds.

When Vampire got home they'd watch TV together. *Sea Hunt*, starring Lloyd Bridges, was the slug's favorite show. Pierre loved the underwater diving and the SCU-BA gear and the magical rising air bubbles. When Pierre's time was up, he left a message written in silvery slime on Vampire's dark desktop. The message was sad and touching, too private to share with you here.

Pierre is above now, or reincarnated into another form. You can trust Vampire on that. That's what vampires know.

On Worship

For the Poet Dante

Vampire was speeding through the West Texas desert, going 95 mph on I-10 east of Fort Stockton, headed for the hot springs in Truth or Consequences, New Mexico, when he slammed on his breaks and stopped to pick up a naked hitchhiker.

"Why are you naked?" Vampire asked.

"Would you believe if I told you I got robbed? They took everything, including my clothes," she answered. "My name's Beatrice. You wouldn't have a cigarette on you?"

They stopped in Fort Stockton to find her cigarettes and something to wear. When the woman got out of his pick-up Vampire realized how fully naked she was. What Vampire means is he could see through her body. One might say her whole body was like a moving open window onto another world.

While she looked through the racks of clothes at the Goodwill, Vampire continued to look through her moving figure. What Vampire saw first was a huge field of sunflowers. Vampire had never been near a large field of sunflowers and tended to see them as rather solitary in twos or threes.

After watching them sway in the breeze Vampire realized what he saw were not flowers at all but green stalky animals with giant yellow eyes. These creatures possessed amazing powers, for they could not only stare directly at the sun but turn to follow the sun's motion through the sky. They all stood silent in mystic adoration of their god, and their god was so powerful that if Vampire looked into the eye of a sunflower, Vampire himself became dizzy with adoration of the divine. Vampire felt a hymn forming in his chest, and almost burst into song, but then began to wonder where the veins and arteries were in this wonderful woman.

"How do you like this dress?" Beatrice asked. "It's all covered with sunflowers."

"I love it," Vampire said, "and you're amazing. If I knew you more, I could almost see myself falling in love."

Poet Writes Another Ekphrastic Poem, This One on Love

She gets on the back of the motorcycle, the painter of giant flowers and skulls, the woman in love with the New Mexico desert who is in her forties in the 1940's. She, Georgia O'Keefe, smiles a world wide smile and there's a starry gap between her front teeth, and it's reported she said, "Why didn't anybody tell me about this before?" as the bike goes spinning out across the desert in a splash of dust.

The woman has no fear. The moment is only joy. You can also see part of the face of the male driver that she holds onto in the photograph. It is not yet time for women on the back to be disturbed that they're not the drivers. Perhaps Georgia has enough control in her life by now. Perhaps the thought has come before but now has vanished. Now, her smile is wide and happy, far away from her former lover, the man who made her famous and broke her heart, photographer Edward Steichen.

Poet Writes to Publisher

I scribble this for you at this late hour, friend,
bent down on my old knobby knees, holding
out all these dusty wrinkled missives from

the strewn lost junkyard of my all too worn
and scratched up bloody pumping heart,
watching that sly blade of yours held high

over my bent, praying head. I know how
the blade moves swift and sharp through
the air with a silent swoosh. I feel as if I've

come into a room filled with albino rodents --
squirrels at most, maybe a few shy guinea
pigs. No one has the clue of why. The secret?

I am the lover Romeo and I don't know the
why of this behavior, I throw my thin white
sheets of poems and tales into the high windy

blank, hoping to remind all moving creatures
of oranges, of emerald forests, of dead rusted
pump jacks, of red leaves born of sandy soil,

the way a small child dances down the aisle
in a store, all the soiled sweet breathings and
beatings of the ebullient swirling human heart.

I've brought these loves to a virtual spot where
you can't smell the sweat or hear my breathing,
or surmise how my singing is afraid of breaking.

Chuck Taylor

Ney

Women are fools to be bothered with housework. Look at me; I sleep in a hammock, which requires no making up. I break an egg and sip it raw. I make lemonade in a glass, and then rinse it, and my housework is done for the day.
— Elizabeth Ney

Poet was a then young man, a horny single young man, and that's how he explains his bookish crushes. Poet is convinced that he would have been much better off if he'd gotten loved more often. If Poet loved a book, he fell in love with the author, and this happened frequently. He'd mail these authors passionate love letters in care of their publishers, pleading with them that they let him drop his life and let him come to be with them. He'd do editing for them. He'd clean house.

Whatever. Just let Poet sit at their brilliant feet.

Poet also had a penchant for dead artists, especially Elizabeth Ney, the sculptor who did the bust of sour old Schopenhauer, and reversed his opinion on women from negative to positive. What a woman, standing next to a block of marble with no power tools nearby because it was the nineteenth century, smacking away at the hard rock with a steel hammer. She and her philosopher husband Edmund — the illegitimate son of a Scottish noble — moved to Georgia to live on a utopian commune. When the commune failed, they bought, for pennies on the dollar after the Civil War, La Llendo, a former plantation near Hempstead, Texas. They were so broke they used old moving crates for furniture.

The neighbors considered the Bohemian Ney family daft. Their son wanted to be a redneck cowboy. He died young and Elizabeth grieved hard blaming herself. As a feminist she never took her husband's last name. Edmund helped found Prairie View A&M. Elizabeth built a sculptor's studio in Austin. Today it's a museum anyone can visit. She sold superb statues to the State of Texas of Sam Houston and Stephen F. Austin. You can see them near the south door of the capital building

Poet loved her. He could not resist strong, brilliant women, at least in the abstract. Poet thought he and Edmund and Elizabeth would make a great philosophical threesome. Poet could bring modern science books, a photo book of Robin's sculpture, and birth control back to their time when he time-travelled there. Elizabeth has started sleeping with her servant stretched out on the floor before the door, to prevent Edmund's midnight trysts. Yes, Poet admired them both. What a life they'd pound and mend.

And guess what? Though Poet never made it back in time to enjoy the genius of Elizabeth, Poet got to live a life as adventurous, and got to know amazing glowing artists, brilliant and mad for life.

Vampire, Like Us All...

...often dreams a different path, of making paintings perhaps, mostly in red, but not using blood because in oxygen blood quickly gets too dark. Since the fashion dictates canvass paintings large, he plans to make his small to be original.

He really wants to paint the laughs and smiles of visionary women, whose skulls he knows can burst with light, whose eyes have turned inside to be a part of another story, far from our current rivers.

Felix Culpa

What if Vampire is Poet, and the only blood he draws he draws to feed his insatiable imagination?

What if the body kissed by fangs for blood is the innocent apple of the earth, the apple made by God for Satan to pick, so poet Eve and poet Adam could learn to suck the sweet and sour of love that spins the planet?

What if it was a mistake made by an inferior angel to order the couple to cover in shame their naked bodies?

What if the poet Eve and the poet Adam ran out of songs to sing after they'd written ten thousand praises to God when back in Eden?

What if back in Eden Eve and Adam couldn't smell or feel the beat of blood? What if now they walk the world with fear and trepidation? What if they hear the gears of war and the banging of the pots made by the starving?

Eve and Adam, free now to multiply, and free to fall where the blood flows freely.

The author's no theologian, but what courageous theolo-

Chuck Taylor

gian might come forward to say the fall might be an act of human heroism?

Nuts and Bolts of Poet

When the donkey gets stuck in the mud, and the peasants can't pull the animal free, it's always Poet who comes strolling along the narrow road, and with his wooing wings of words, played like a flute off his tongue, causes the donkey to fall in love again somehow with his laborious life, and step free.

Poets ambles around the night with all his body a luminous firefly. Poet streaks through the day's cruel invisible. With the spin of a word off the tongue, Poet can turn a sinful book holy, or a holy book sinful.

When an odd man haunts the corner and whispers "sinner" as Poet heads for the door, Poet catches the word like a feather in his fingers, and then folds the word into a passionflower. Poet turns, smiles, and offers back to the man his sin.

On the other hand, it is always Poet's bike that breaks down in the race. It is always Poet who burns the frozen pizza in the oven. It is always Poet who makes a wrong turn and puts you at least a hundred miles from your destination.

And it's always Poet, too, who must go back to the first room to remember why he went into the second room, but then must find the room before the first room, to learn the why of why.

It's always Poet who stops in the smaller towns with old-fashioned hardware stores still flourishing, where he can go inside and open small wooden drawers with white knobby handles, to wonder like a Saint Frances at all the different nuts and bolts.

Poet could buy you a matching nut and bolt for a nickel, to wear in your lovely tresses as a silver flower.

Vampire Tries Another Poem called "Life: or, in Vietnam there are Inside and Outside Dogs"

And each dog acts as if it loves its master
And each dog knows what kind of dog it is

It's the inside dog's luck is to be petted and pampered
It's he outside dog's luck to receive the dinner scraps

The inside dog knows the warmth of the night fire
The outside dog knows the rain and raging cold

The inside dog plans to die a ripe and ancient age
The outside ripens to cower and then be eaten

The inside dog fetches many a sock in his dreams
The outside whimpers recalling the stick and beatings

The inside knows the best of all possible worlds
The outside rages inside, of love still dreaming.

Now that's Reporting!

Poet has been putting his socks on! It feels as if he were unrolling mountains onto his feet! Now he is taking in the soil of distant and mysterious lands whose languages he will never know, drinking his morning cup of Joe! The sunlight streams in the kitchen window unaware of the concept of property, not bothering to ring the doorbell!

Wouldn't you know? As expected, Puritanism has flexed its muscles and returned as strong as ever! And we thought we'd vanished the Man in Black to a small atoll in the South Pacific, where the women go topless, the men wear loincloths, and everyone worships volcanoes!

Be restrained, Puritan says! Don't like the erotic! Don't show excitement unless it's necessary to feign at the close of a sale! *The New York Times*, hardly restrained in its war coverage, likes to believe it's restrained in its style!

The paper's gone sober, and so has banned exclamation points! The ghost of Little Orphan Annie is sobbing! You can't, it seems, be exuberant and write the truth at the same time! Poet says to go ahead, and when necessary, let things smoke at the edges, or set them burning!

Much Ado about Much Ado

Vampire himself has never seen a congregation of alligators, not in the water anyway. They seem lone wolves. When apes get together you get a shrewdness that can outsmart any flange of baboons or battery of barracudas. Vampire believes he has more culture contained in his cuticle than any culture of bacteria, than any football culture or baseball culture, and Vampire could howl better than a band or coyotes, better than any cackle of hyenas or scold of jays. Vampire's normal voice could scare off a scourge of mosquitoes, a plague of locusts, or a murder of crows. But Vampire did once get into a pickle of porcupines, after being chased by a coterie of prairie dogs. Poor Vampire looked worse than a wreck of seabirds. He had to get off his bed of clams and join a run of salmon, and with the wisdom of wombats and a zeal of zebras, herd buffalo into a congress of salamanders that got Vampire to a lounge of lizards filled with loving chatter like a charm of goldfinches. After the chatter the lizards led Vampire safely to a lovely litter of pooping puppies, where the dark creature could rest and heal, and later join a romp of otters that acted like a pomp of Pekinese and an exultation of skylarks. Vampire, after all that, talked of joining an army of ants or maybe a caravan of camels. His Darkness liked the rumba of rattlesnakes, but short

Chuck Taylor

of cash, he briefly settled down with a family of human sardines commuting to Houston in the corporate of work.

Poet's "Breath of my Breath"

I loved you because it was the season of owls
    and buttercups
I loved you because of the post oaks that shaded
    the door of your long-gone apartment
I love you because of the collapsing fence
    with dusty ivy covered
I could see out the kitchen window in the hour
    of dishes

I loved you because of the tight trim of your
    cornrow hair
I loved you because you would not wear gold jewelry
    as long as there were people walking poor
    the streets,
I loved you for your water filtration systems we later
    stored on a pallet in my garage
I loved you because your telephone reigned with rings
the day and night with orders for vitamins
    and supplements

Love that did not mind the upside-down of words
    in the rough winds of strained and tired evenings
Love that grew thin at times when too long we cursed
    together the bitter wages of the world

Chuck Taylor

Love that put on weight in the hummingbird night
    of our sheets and arms,
Love that grew long hair glowing in the long lazy
    afternoons of slumbering campfires
Love that could be set on an anvil and pounded into
    ductile sheets
Love that moved like water between wildflowers
    tiny alive in the rarefied cracks of cement
Love that made me later lie and lie to the man calling to
    repossess your car

I worshipped at the halo of your nipples
I worshipped the shape of your front teeth
I worshipped the hairline of your fractures
I worshipped the tongue of your mouth meeting
    the lips of words

You were brewed from mountain springs
You were brewed from the rocket of semen
    and the rejecting and blessing egg
You were brewed from the sensuous porches
    and the singing of field-dappled crickets

There now, my hand exploring the textures
    of your eyebrow
There now, my hand exploring the under arch of your
    left foot
There now, my tongue exploring a lobe of your ear
There now, my nose smelling the deep cities of your
    Self that I so often travelled,
though I yearn now to caress with the wind of hands
    and words the street-lit cities of your eminent skin

You know that we lived from one word to another
    in words,
like aphrodisiac teas by the cedars in the still
    and naked night

You know that the words we spoke lived in the air
    of time
You know that love is a god who visits in the air of time
You know I have constructed an altar inside my words
and that altar—this poem—is made from the smoke
    of words remembering

I loved you because of the sunlight off your skin
I loved you because you worked the streets of my
    loneliness
I loved you because of your nostrils and your bent toes
    of high-heeled shoes
I loved you because of the simple ache in my heart
    to kiss your moonlit collarbone
I loved you rolling and still
I loved you transcending and I loved you somnolent
    in the humid breath of summer night

I hear your breathing still in my breath after breath
I taste your words in the cavities of my worried bones

Those words smacking from the mountains of your lips
    like divine wind
Those words around the muscle flexing of your
    consonants
Those words around the blues and blessing
    of your vowels

You, always breathing in the flight of words,
Words that were the breath that called my clay to love
Words that took from my rib and filled me
    with the beasts of tenderness
Words that parted my seas in seven days
    by the seven ways
Words that brought down the from the mountain
    the commandments

Chuck Taylor

I yearned to break and fulfill,
Words that brought me shaking to frail knees
Words that drove me from the room and called me
    back again and again

Oh, I still hear you in my breathing
Oh, I still see the intonations of your smile
    on the sidewalks of day and night
Oh, I still hear the rip of your shoulder turning
    and lifting,
the sway of your hips as you make your way
down your own lighted and separate path

Oh I knew you,
I knew you for a time
in the air of time
granted by the god of love in time

I knew you
breathing
as I breathe
in and out
the day and night

Where is Captain Marvel?

Has he moved on to the gorgeous Atlas Mountains, say, deep in the interior of Algeria? Perhaps he lives in a small adobe hut on a Greek island, and in that hut he has a five foot tall earthen jar filled with olives, and he's been subsisting on those olives and making his way through the great big books, titles like *The Tale of Genji*, *Remembrance of Things Past*, *The Brothers Karamazov*, and *War and Peace*.

He could be slightly miffed at all these years it's taken to put him up on the silver screen. What did they do before? Invent the totally irredeemable Iron Man. Vampire says, so what if Captain Marvel's a cheap knock-off Superman. We can't put Superman up on the silver screen because we're mourning for Christopher Reeves, who was Superman. Bring in the second string. Let him read Nietzsche like Batman did, so he can acquire a dark side and be more interesting.

The audience can discover something new about Captain Marvell if the rights to the film are given to an avant-garde artist instead of a boring mainstream director. Maybe Marvel's a polygamist with three wives and eighteen kids. These films play fast and footloose with all the comic book characters anyway. Remember when Superman got to smooch with Lois Lane? Suppose Captain Marvell is a vampire. He's caught a woman midair that jumped out of a high-rise building to kill herself. Should he bite and suck her blood, have a little feast as he swoops around in space?

Maybe so.

After all, she was going to die anyway.

Or better yet, suppose Captain Marvel isn't a guy who's gay but a woman with superpowers. The movie's set in the 1950's when there were no opportunities for women, and so she had to pass as a man to have success. Now there's a plotline for you. Make her a daughter of Hera. That should bring "him" out of the Atlas Mountains.

Tragic, Comic

Poet wants this prose poem to be funny but his brain's fried from too much partying and he can't recall, at the moment, a single joke. Usually Poet's got as many jokes on him as a can of pickup stick cans holds sticks, but his soul's as parched as Nevada.

Maybe things are going to turn tragic around here. What if Poet said he was turning into an alcoholic? Maybe it's not the brain that's in trouble but the liver. If he keeps this drinking up, the cost of Scotch alone will put him on the streets, down on Chicago's Skid Row, standing under an elevated train in the middle of winter warming his hands over a metal trash barrel.

It'll go down to fifteen below some night, and the mission won't take Poet inside because he can't walk the line to prove himself sober. Maybe the alcohol in his blood will act like anti-freeze? There's some hope. Or maybe Poet can call his son and he'll come and get him, let Poet sleep on the couch. So what if son's wife gets mad. Poet is the father here. That should be worth something.

Wait a minute.

Reader, do you know why Cinderella was never good at

soccer? It's because she's always running away from the ball.

Reader, do you recall when Poet was a kid and wanted to be a magician? He was always sawing people in two. That's why he has a half daughter.

And Reader, where do vampires keep their savings accounts? In blood banks, of course. You know, Reader, my vampire girlfriend broke up with me. I wasn't her type.

Tongue

Poet has been biting his tongue lately, and he thinks that it's some kind of sign.

Through most of his life, he'd bite his tongue about once every five years. It's amazing when you think about it, the duck and dance of the tongue around your teeth, it's tender flesh trying to avoid a bite and cut from the rows and rows of hard, sharp incisors.

No one ever takes the time to thank his or her tongue for its bravery in a dangerous situation, as well as for its amazing agility. The tongue is like the woman tied to the wall, holding cards in her hands and teeth. The sharpshooter rides by on his stallion and sends the bullet into the two aces in her hands, and then they turn the wall so she's sideways and he shoots the last card out from between her teeth. I never understood why the sharpshooter got all the credit.

Think of it. It's what your tongue does automatically for you day in and night out, through all your endless talking, your gluttonous eating, and your loud snoring, without once getting credit. That's one amazing little mouse you've got there.

Chuck Taylor

But Poet, his tongue was all beaten up. Was he talking too fast? Was he eating too fast? Was he not paying attention? Perhaps the tongue felt ignored and wanted to show him what happens when you forget an essential part.

Poet started eating slower. Poet started speaking slower. He did his best for his tongue. Since he couldn't leave his tongue at the hospital, he relied on self-treatment.

He told his tongue. "I will not lie. I will not say hurtful words to others. I will try to give people strength and courage in the face of the life's atrocious difficulties with my healing words and poems. I will tell those I love that I love them. I will say encouraging words to my friends. I will make people laugh. I will not talk to Vampire even if he's on the next page. Vampires, with their fangs, must need to be extra careful not to injure their tongues. The pain of a bitten tongue is constantly annoying, and those bites can hurt as bad as an earache. The human tongue is no turtle—that's for sure. It's got no shell to duck inside and hide.

"I will say prayers to my tongue, who is part of God, and I will say prayers to Jesus, who is the divine not in me, and I will say prayers to my ancestors for giving me the gift of the tongue to talk and sing and say my poems out loud."

Dear Readers, if you have problems with your tongue, say it turns forked or blue or swollen or something, feel free to try some of the things I've suggested here. Do not take my words, in any manner or form, as tongue in cheek.

Vampire Says

Poet, you need to find an old rock wall.
Poet, I'm telling you, study how it holds
back miles and miles of heavy earth.

Poet, take a look at its infinite crevices.
Poet, observe the cracks in its mortar.
Poet, do you see? Worlds of lives live

there so you must stare through time,
through seasons humid and freezing,
through the falling leaves and bald sun.

Poet, please, tell us nothing of yourself,
for your soul is no more interesting than
a nasty swarm of buzzing mosquitoes.

Poet, we need and grow hungry to hear,
desperate and lovely on the lonely page,
the deep and festive music of the wall.

Chuck Taylor

Vampire on the Bus

Vampire gets deeply nostalgic at times for the elderly women on Dallas buses, sitting up close to the driver, singing their Christian hymns. Most riders avoid them and see them as insane. Vampire thought they were the sanest ones, and what courage, to sing so loudly in their squeaky, out of tune, quavering old voices on a public bus!

Vampire later had a job on the Salt Lake City buses helping commuters find empty seats to survive the crushed commute as they heading into town for work. In Utah the rich, the middle, and the poor ride the buses. This bus system practices democracy.

Vampire had to wrap an arm around a pole up front to keep from falling over on some of the quick turns the bus made. He tried to shout some jokes out loud to make the trip more enjoyable, but doubted most of the people in the back could hear. Vampire had his jokes memorized, and he only did "up" jokes. He felt it was depressing enough having to go to work so early in the morning. Vampire rode many long routes into Salt Lake City from the various distant suburbs so the riders did not have to hear his memorized jokes over and over. He had about twenty "up" jokes memorized.

Vampire was envious of the Dallas bus hymnists because they sat down and faced the front of the bus. They sang mostly for themselves, and did not care if anyone listened. Vampire, when working the buses of Salt Lake City, often seethed with resentment because so few riders put their newspapers down to give him attention.

"Look you creeps," he was tempted to shout, "the city bus system is paying me two thousand a month to do this. I am a well-known entertainer! I've appeared in numerous vampire "B" movies at drive in movie theatres across our great country." Vampire thought the passengers were rude and he had the urge to slide up next to them and take a nip or two from some of the prettier necks, but that would get him both arrested and fired, and now he needed the money.

To hold onto his cool, Vampire always remembered the Dallas hymnists. They knew that God was listening, and that was enough.

Chuck Taylor

Dinosaur Dance

Poet at times gets the idea stuck in his head, fair or unfair, that a certain machine has taken on a personal dislike for him. People do that. Horses do that. Why not machines? Poet doesn't know why. He hasn't, to the best of his knowledge, done anything or said anything to offend the machine. It could be chemistry. He does know that cars have tried to run him over.

Recently for Poet, it was the washing machine. The tension quickly grew thicker than a steam sauna when Poet entered the laundry room. Poet felt like he was inside a bag of marbles. Every time he used the machine, the washer would start its angry banging and dinosaur dance across the floor, no matter how carefully Poet balanced around its pole the whites and colors. Poet tried all the settings on the machine's dashboard but none of them helped. One afternoon Poet found one of his Siamese cats trapped inside, the lid closed, the poor animal wrung out and nearly dead.

Who knows? Maybe some washing machines are in training for the next life, where they'll be vampires.

A Great Taboo Exists...

...concerning the method of vampire conception. Poet has brought you here to sweep away that darkness. Poet knows to some it may be a delicate subject. They'd rather the knowledge remain hidden in order to maintain a frightening mystery, the pretense that vampires are created out of humans by a mere bite.

Mating between male and female vampires is quick and almost brutal, like that between any raptors in the air. The blood of one vampire is poisonous to another so they don't bite and suck each other. It's a genetic mutation that guarantees the survival of the species.

Vampires are marsupials, and once the female lays her eggs, she puts them in a pouch on her belly. The reason so few vampires exist is due to the fact that the eggs are a prized delicacy to the woodland fox—a shy, rarely seen animal that actually has a range of many continents.

Like any species, the vampire, with such a clever natural enemy, becomes highly vulnerable. In that way the vampire is kind of kin—another one of the hunted--and is open to some sympathy, though limited. Marsupials have become somewhat rare. Given that vampires are marsupials, they probably originated in Australia, not Romania, as the old Hollywood horror films seem to want us to believe.

Bicycles

Vampire has never been good at lying, but he's been practicing in front of a mirror. Finally he goes to his favorite bar, sits down next to a woman who is by herself, and orders both of them margaritas for starters.

"You can tell I'm a vampire, I suppose, says Vampire. "Well, I am in love with you, and because I love you so deeply, I promise I will never bite you and suck your blood."

"Prove it," says the lady. "Show me your fangs."

"I will," says the Vampire, "but first you have to flash me one of your boobs."

"I can't do that in a public place," says the woman. She reaches in her purse for a cigarette, and then remembers you can't smoke in bars anymore, so she pulls out a tick-tack. She takes one out of the plastic box and offers it to the Vampire. "I am working on a PhD in biochemistry," she says. "I know a lot about DNA, and I don't believe in vampires."

"No thanks—for the tick tack," says Vampire. "Refined

sugar is not part of a vampire's diet. It could cause me to pass out."

"Well why not?" says the woman. "People pass out here all the time. The bartenders can handle it."

"Point taken," replies Vampire, "but I can't risk flashing my fangs. I realize now you could be Buffy for all I know. That would explain my irresistible attraction to you."

"Who?"

"You know. The Slayer. Of Vampires."

"But that's fiction, a TV show."

"It always felt to me to have aspects of a documentary."

"Well … anyways, look: I don't have blonde hair."

"You could have dyed it, to go better undercover—or be wearing a wig."

"I suppose that's your way of flattering me, telling me I'm beautiful."

"Yes. You don't have a sword, do you? Say back in your car."

"No, but I have a mace in my purse."

"That stuff has no effect on a vampire."

"How are you surviving, without blood, I mean."

"It's not the most tasty, but a sampling of large lizards

can do in a pinch. I first got the idea on a trip to Mexico."

"You drink the blood of lizards?"

"I told you I was a vampire. I'm in love with you. I've been observing you here at this bar for over a month. I suppose you could call me a stalker vampire, but to honor you, my love, I've sworn off people for the time being.

"Well, vampire, I guess the most important thing is that you use a condom."

"No problem. But of course you realize I'm a virgin. You are my first and only human love. For you, I have filed down my fangs. They're not sharp anymore. I'll show you when we get to your car—the holes I mean. Just promise me you're not Buffy."

"What about your car? Why my car?"

"Vampires don't need cars. If we're not flying, we walk or ride bicycles."

My Friend

It's astounding. It's precious. Poet can't hold off any longer telling you about the white and blue flowers that sit in the middle of a modest table in a small canning glass at the Village Café in Bryan.

You know it's his madness that makes him tell you.

This, that's glorious, won't be here that long. Ah, such a miracle. The sun's rays stretch in from the front windows twenty feet away and kiss these flowers. Not the whole table, just the flowers and the glass that holds them. The long horizontal rays of the setting sun can pull off miracles like that.

The sunlight makes the glass glow and the flowers a brilliant scarlet and white, intense with beauty. Poet gets up for a closer look—primroses and Queen Anne's lace -- he'd guess, picked he figures out of a nearby vacant lot.

Poet is so in the moment, and he is mad with happiness. His feet are shouting at his body to do a little blissful dance, but Poet is shy and doesn't want the customers in the café to know of his exhilaration.

But now that Poet has finished telling you, dear friend, the light has faded. Yet that moment, that small splendor remains under our skin, if you like. It lives here on this page, and lives, Poet hopes, in you.

It's gone from the world forever, but will always be with us, and for anyone who wishes to find again, right here.

Always You Consider the Weather

It's a good day to die. No, maybe it's not such a good day. Maybe it's an OK day to die, or a negative day, or even a shameful day for dying. All you ask of death is the right weather.

Someone—maybe it was Shakespeare or Sitting Bull, or Dustin Hoffman in *Little Big Man*—spoke the above-mentioned immortal line about mortality. These dudes were then in great health, bright plums of happiness in the sun, satisfied as a sleepy cat with the quality of their lives, as they stared down on stage a man-eating lion, or looked over the ridge at the rifles on the other side.

Maybe Hollywood directors ordered their writers to put the line in films because Indians were always dying and the directors didn't want the primarily white audiences to feel guilty about the ethnic cleansing carried out by settlers, small pox blankets, forced marches, and by the US Calvary.

Today is not a good day to die as far as Poet is concerned. It's cold and the roads are icy slick. The hearse, not pulled by a horse, could slide off the road or get in a wreck carrying his body in such a slippery season to the dim and flowered funeral home.

Let Poet check his appointment book and call you back on that. Perhaps Poet has an hour free at three AM in 2043, while lying cozy in bed, cuddling next to his main squeeze, an insouciant Minnesota summer breeze bustling through the dry green leaves outside—but we could take a rain check on that. A good day to die should not be a dry kind of day, but a good hair kind of day, with clean underpants.

Drano

Vampire liked to imagine he was the sleek art deco Bela Lugosi type of vampire from the 1930's black and white cinema. His literary model, less important but still influential, was Bram Stoker's 1897 classic, Count Dracula.

Vampire loved it when during the night the moon, the trees, the shrubbery, and even the house, seemed to play along with his Bela Lugosi fantasies.

And here he was at the open window in his black tuxedo, and there she was stretched out under filmy sheets in the moonlight, her lovely long red hair splayed across the pillow, her long white neck and tender shoulders naked, just waiting for his kiss.

Vampire imagines his teeth penetrating her carotid artery was like a needle being set down on an old Victrola to play Mozart.

But then it happened. No blood flowed up into his fangs, and he had to pull to dislodge them. And then no red blood flooded out of her neck onto the sheets. Vampire touched the woman's arm. It was cold. He stroked her perfect skin; it was smooth, very smooth, but also hard.

Vampire scraped the woman's skin with his fingernail and held her hand up for a closer look and smelled it.

The white sliver on his nail, it was wax. This was not an embalmed woman but a lovely lass, stolen perhaps from Madame Tussaud's Wax Museum in Paris, or could it be that whatever man had loved this gorgeous woman could not bear to part with her image, and commissioned the all too perfect replica from Madame Tussaud's? Where is that man, in the bedroom next door?

Vampire was both horrified and disgusted. And to make matters worse, his fangs were now clogged with wax. He searched his black tuxedo for a toothpick, or a pocket-knife, to get the wax out of his fangs, but what would a tuxedo be doing carrying such uncouth objects?

To the Reader

Poet wishes to be with a person who somehow has remained vulnerable, open to the world. Eros is not the issue, but it is crucial they be together heart to heart, that they tell stories and try to love a little one another, and then to sleep and sleep and move into a kind of holy animal oneness.

Sometimes Poet despairs. So many stunning stories wait off back roads and even at Interstate roadside stops. They almost cry for a hearing, yet time evaporates like winter snowmelt. Poet wants to know whole encyclopedias of dreams, in the downbeat and upbeat of syllables, as well as the quiet faces in their questions of prayer. Are we to go to death forever naïve and ignorant, cut off from all this splendid heartache and flowering?

Time does gallop, like clouds on a windy day. Please, Poet needs you here just to talk, to hold hands and admire all the lovely divergent routes. Poet needs your attention, and needs to give attention. Imagine we are strangers sharing a seat on a long train ride across this wide American continent.

Poet's "Ut Pictora Poesis'

This sonnet has large flat areas of color,
a pomegranate scarlet, a banana yellow,
a blueberry blue, and since this sonnet
imitates the works of the painter Mondrian,
there are no people on the page—no lover
or bank teller, no large animals with enormous
love calls, no soft sunrises over mobile homes
and no common shells gleaming in the sand
one might scoop up; this is a minimalist song
and may not even make fourteen; you must
give up on that, just bathe in the pure color
running over your hands, color so arranged
like a friendly chat among the best of friends

Screw the Sanitation, Life is More than Dry Cleaning

Why is it when Poet watches the men coming home from war on TV, the wives are always slim and trim with perfect teeth and clean and perfect hair? The men come rolling off the C-47's in fresh pressed uniforms, cleanly shaved, with big smiles and swelling happy chests.

Is this a movie set? They certainly act like movie stars. The lightning is perfect. The tears flow at the right moment for the cameras. Barbee Barbie and Barbie Ken—out of his GI Joe combat gear—run into each other's arms, like Juliet and Romeo, as if the miles and months of distance can be swept away like dust. And then the children and babies, there's no holding back. They hug their warriors with perfect bright and shinning faces.

That's not the way his kids behaved when Poet had been gone a week. They looked at Poet with crossed eyes. Their body language said they were hurt and mad, and wondered where and why Poet had been gone.

Now don't get me wrong. Poet is glad to see the soldiers home. Poet is glad everyone's loving each other. Crying is good. Hugging is good. May all these marriages last a thousand years; may there be no soldier suicides. May there be no one missing legs or arms. May each soldier on his final tour step into a stable job because America's companies are grateful to these men who have saved access to middle eastern oil to keep our turbines turning, and kept us worker bees in factories free from terrorist bombings.

Oh yeah, Poet wants the best for them, but Poet doesn't like being lied to. The truth can bite at times, but then at times we need to bleed. We civilians watching TV news may be ten thousand miles away, but we know war's monster pain and ugliness creeps like a vampire down our streets and around our doors every moment of the day and night.

Killer

With enough forgetfulness and training, even a killer can write a decent prose poem. Some blood will spill on the page, perhaps, but can be chased away when the poem is typed up. Poet is a killer like Vampire. He does some killing every day—mostly to eat—and it bothers him more and more as we learn more about animal intelligence.

You'd think with all the schools of fish Poet's eaten, the wisdom would have worked its way into his DNA, and he'd be better at the creature dance, that he could move more with his sisters and brothers—the hundreds of schools of fish and birds—turning right, turning left, together, with no choreography or rehearsals.

And yes, Poet's murdered others—maybe fifty white rats doing experiments in hospital laboratories, in order to complete research that might save lives. He was following his uncle's advice, training to become a brain surgeon. Poet has killed dogs helping surgeons learn how to perform open-heart surgery. He fainted once in the middle of an operation. Blood flew everywhere and should be in these words and on this page. Poet once had a dog let out a moan and die licking his fingers, after they tied him down and drained out all his blood, to use in the practice of open-heart surgery by young surgeons. That dog was Jesus.

There are days Poet wants to bang his head against the wall, days he wants to put his head in an oven. Poet's dreams have never been good, and he learned from them so many ways to curse himself.

What hope for one like Poet, except to practice kindness, kindness, kindness, compassion and kindness...

Paradox

Poet recalls the paradox, how to save her—the one who filled his soul to amazement—he had to leave her. She'd grown to hate him. Her hatred seemed a mineral pain that couldn't be dissolved by the waters of forgiveness, and like a vampire it sucked him dry. In one of her finest tales a guy who looks and acts like Poet gets sliced and diced with a knife.

Yes, Poet had to leave her, because of hatred impervious to alteration. How she rode that hatred, no doubt justified; how she had to disagree with whatever he said; how it was pushing them into such terrible corners. They'd grown to be poorer than poverty.

What he suggested was imaginative and practical, but she had to disagree, and then when he did leave her finally, all fell into place in a few short years. She did spend some time living on the street, but forgot he'd said they needed to move to the country; forgot he'd explained they couldn't afford the rents in the city. In the country they could grow food, they could keep chickens, live in a mobile home.

Yes, she forgot how she'd said she'd never ever leave

her trendy city, how she'd never live in a trashy mobile home—words she fired from the stone battery of her hatred became, by the magic of forgetfulness, her own words, and now she's got a lovely mobile home. Now she has a wide garden and chickens on country land she loves to stroll, and all one can do is hope that Courtney's at last free and happy.

Entertaining Babies

For K

Poet, always Protestant and practical, will now attempt the topic of babies and their entertainment, even though Poet is old and hasn't been around those pampers for a while. You may not have babies now, but chances are you will be around babies in the future, SO PAY ATTENTION! Not often do you get self-help from Poet.

You're not at home where splayed about the floor live happy baby toys. You are trying to save ten bucks by paying for your motor vehicle registration at the county building. You're in a long line, full of inchworms impatiently blocked and slowly moving. You've got the kid in a sling up front so the baby faces toward you, but of course the baby's bored with your mug and wants to take on the world, yet the kid still needs your protection. The beast counts on your protection, but will not admit it except by the eyes.

Things you've already done to entertain the beast: (1) Bouncing, (2) Face mugging, (3) Making strange beeps, hums, and whistles, (4) Pointing at various objects and repeating the word, like you were an ESL teacher—floor, window, light, ceiling—etc. (5) Tickling, and (6) Pretending to eat the baby's hand.

O but the beast wants down. You can't let the babe go far because you'll lose your place in line. These are grim and tired inchworms. They won't let you back in if you stray too far. You can give the baby your keys to mouth and drool on. You can take out important things from your wallet and let your baby pull out the plastic cards and try to put them back, greased down with spit. A smart person will have a sheet of paper and a pen so the baby can make precious abstract art while sitting on the shabby floor. You can put the baby on your shoulders, turn around and bounce gently, holding the baby's hands. You can stand sideways in the line and with two hands under baby's arms swing the beastie up and down between your legs.

ARE YOU TAKING NOTES? YOU WILL, IN THE FUTURE, NEED THIS STUFF. Hopefully some of this is deep in your memory banks from when you were a baby and your mother and father waited in the same kind of persnickety line.

ARE YOU HAVING FUN YET? You should be having fun. Being in line with a baby to entertain is better than being in line alone. The little beastie's smiles, the little beastie's giggles, the movement of beast eyes and hands can be more fun than video games—or all night moshing. There's a joy to be had if you're into joy and know where joy sleeps and how to roust her out. Baby makes things new. The dusty old county building's a miracle. Your billfold is more amazing than Michelangelo's ceiling at the Vatican.

If the line is long and slow enough, your imagination will

have to strain for other ways to please your beast. Poet's a guy, and pretty eccentric. His pants don't fall down easily, so he pulls off his belt and puts it around the baby under the arms and swings the baby more, around in a circle. The line doesn't mind. The baby will want to sit on the floor and taste the metal and leather of the belt. What else? You got some Chap Stick? Beasts love to eat Chap Stick and watch it go up and down like lipstick. Perhaps, if you're totally amazing and poetic, you've got on hand a wand and plastic bottle with soapy water to blow bubbles. * God, you're going to need to stretch your imagination.

The sun is setting and Poet's still in line. That's all right. Poet didn't get here till three in the afternoon. It's December and the sun slides to bed early. Poet's running out of inventions and hoping the baby's about to fall asleep. The beast is growing cranky and fussing. The beast wants more of the world. The beast sees people coming in and out glass doors. The beast points and points and wants to go out. The beast throws the head back and pushes to get out of your arms. You bounce the beast. You say shush and shush and you give your beast kisses on the neck that get a few giggles, but soon the beast is full blown crying. The beast is revving up the vocal chords. The beast could sing opera. Wine glass breaking with a high C is nothing for the beast.

So what do you do? Not much. You try a few more tricks. You bounce and kiss and say shush, you follow the Buddha and keep your emotions disengaged. You do the itsy bitsy spider with one hand, sing "Old McDonald had a Farm,"* but the beast is out to determine limits of power, pushing to see how far it can go, but you're bigger and the beast can't win. Poet knows the kid is tired. Baby can keep Poet up at night, but the wailing will slow and cease, so cool it and don't let the screech owl love get under your skin. You're not at some lecture or concert. The inch-worms in line can handle the noise. The beast is pooped but won't admit to it. Baby may poop and fall asleep half way through a one-syllable word.

Finally you reach the end of the line. It's two minutes to five. The lady behind the glass gives you a tired smile and slides a sucker under the glass for baby. The baby sees the bright red and perks up.

* Suggested by Larry Heinemann
* Suggested by Linda Donan

Faith

There's a side of old Vampire that wants to see people holding their bibles up toward the sky, like they stand on street corners holding their cell phones, waiting for the light to change.

One thing's for certain, God doesn't have a cell phone and he won't be fingering you up, sending an email or texting a message. Vampire knows the gods prefer the rocky peaks of mountains. Gods speak out of the whirlwind.

Now Jesus, the carpenter, well, he's a different kind of character. You could find him with a crew at a construction site, building wall frames for HUD homes.

Filing Cabinet on Your Back

He often forgets they are there, but once and a while he will stop and ask, 'Why and how long have I carried this three drawer metal filing cabinet?' Poet has to carry the file of his wife's on and off ups and downs. Poet has to carry the file on the daughter in Brooklyn barely making ends meet as a waitress, the file on the son who at forty-five has learned finally that most dreams don't come true, and the file on the trucker son hauling hazardous wastes across the wide dark night. Poet has a file on his father's alcoholism. Poet has the file of his shut-in mother's suicide attempts and his aunt and sister's stays in mental hospitals.

The filing cabinet's metal edges dig into the back. The poor down the street at the shelter, Poet feels them too and makes donations. The crazy man that once was a lawyer and lost his family in a fire, Poet feels him and sits at times with him where he sits each day in front of Pete's Pizza. The fate of the Republic, Poet carries that and often weeps. Poet almost died of cancer and carries a scar from his navel to his throat. The filing cabinet on the back, it's lighter than what millions are carrying up steeper hills. Where would he be without it? Poet wouldn't be himself—that's for sure—and Poet wouldn't be so attached, so in love with the here and now of the daily groaning blooms of life.

For Wallace Stevens

The only emperor is the emperor wiping down the café tables and filling up the heavy Porcelain white coffee cups of farmers. The only emperor is the graduate student behind the bar, serving up till late at night the foaming drafts of fifty brands of beer in frosty mugs. The only emperor is the sweaty boy of the tire shop who pulled the nail and patched Poet's tire as good as new in less that an hour. The only emperor is the single mother ringing up Poet's light bulb purchase at the checkout counter in the General Dollar. The only emperor is renting a movie out of a metal box for her boyfriend. A bag of groceries for cooking supper sits at her feet. Over her cell phone she asks her boyfriend what kind of film he'd like to watch. The only emperor has the courage to remove her clothes at the Yellow Rose on Lamar, dancing slow and exhausted around a pole. She's hardened and barely can recall she once liked men, but she's reminding men of the love of a woman's touch that they hunger for and wish to never forget. The only emperor works at the Dairy Queen. All week her lungs have hurt and Poet's suggested some of his grandmother's remedies. She's fixing him a senior softy ice cream cone dipped in melted chocolate for a dollar, and whispers, "This one's on the house."

Here We Are

You could be a homerun baseball, blasted out of the stadium by a Berry Bonds, steroid type slugger, lying obscure in the grass some five seasons now and no fan has picked you up to take you home.

Vampire spots you on one of his wandering pointless evening strolls, and puts you in his pocket. Vampire hopes you recover from the pounding you endured at the plate. He hopes the rain hasn't rotted your insides, and that the blazing sun didn't fray too bad your skin.

You're not alone, and must know that this world can't be called your fault.

In the Hurricane

Georgia found a dusty tape under their bed. She popped it in the cassette player in the living room, standing by the large glass windows, looking out on a drizzly April day and at their empty swimming pool. On the tape she heard her husband Tony making love to his former wife, now married to a man wealthier than they'd ever be. Georgia recognized every groan her Tony made. She had a secret stash of cash squirreled away from the grocery money he'd given her. Georgia didn't know how to drive a car, so she had to call a taxi, after she packed, in order to leave the man.

That was twenty-five years ago when they lived in Dallas. They're in Houston now and still together. Georgia's only daughter, from her first marriage, lives with them, along with the daughter's children.

* * *

Jamie got a call from her former husband. He was up Interstate 35 forty-seven miles holed up in a motel in Austin. The woman he'd tried to make it with was in the parking lot talking on her cell phone. Michael had some kind of reaction to the Viagra he'd taken. He couldn't sit still and had red spots all over his skin. His head felt like a ticking terrorist bomb. Jamie drove up from San Antonio, calmed him down, and made him drink a lot of water to piss the drug from his system.

They'd been divorced less than a year. Now they've been back together ten years. She works in the probation office for the state. He's due to retire from being a dentist.

All the clichéd tales of broken hearts, all the bloody tales of revenge—we don't need to slide around in that rut anymore, and they're easy to put down in tragic words. Those that hang on in the hurricane, hold on with hungry hearts and make forgiveness, they're the ones that interest Poet, perhaps because he can not do it.

Just About Evil, Just About Love

Poet is an American of the suburban middle class, and as a consequence has been fortunate–or perhaps unfortunate–not to have experienced much contact with evil. Poet was born toward the end of World War II and grew up during the forties and fifties. By the time the turbulent sixties arrived his values were set and he passed through those exciting but dangerous times changed but unharmed. His values were quiet streets and lawns, the reliable delivery of the mail, a multitude of cats and dogs in and out of the home, knowing a neighbor or two, the doors unlocked because of no fear of robbery, the freedom to wander small undeveloped tracks of woods, and to dream—walking the railroad tracks over small rivers crossed by steel trestles—of adventures in far and grand mysterious places. Poet avoided the Vietnam war by being in college at the right time, getting married at the right time, having children at the right time, and becoming a teacher at the right time. By the time they tried to draft Poet he'd developed varicose veins in his right leg and was declared unfit for service under current standards.

Poet has read books on evil taking up many topics—the holocaust and the Armenian genocide, for instance—and while the reading sickened him and ruined his sleep for days and made him even more anti-war, he has never had to participate in great evil directly, or been the victim of great evil. He knows that there are people nearby who exist that will quickly fire workers and spread rumors to ruin their reputations, but Poet has remained anonymous, a small bug hidden under a rock, and has been mostly untouched. Poet would however like to relate two small incidents, out of many, where he came into contact with persons who might have perpetuated evil.

The first event occurred when Poet was driving back to his job in Galveston from Dallas, Texas, in 1979 along Interstate 45, after a weekend visit with family. Poet was driving a camper truck—an old one—whose wheels would get stuck in the groves large trucks create in the cement pavement of freeways. His vehicle would swerve in those grooves made by larger sets of tires, or swerve when Poet tried to extricate his wheels from the grooves.

A police car in Webster noticed the swerving, and pulled Poet over. Noticing his long hair and beard, the officers asked him if he was smoking pot and had marijuana in his vehicle. Poet said he did not. While one officer guarded him, the other got inside his vehicle and started ripping apart the camper with its drawers and bed and cabinets, searching for any hidden drugs. Before he had done too much damage, a car suddenly went by going perhaps a hundred and ten miles an hour. The police officer guarding him said with a smirk, "This is your lucky day," and the two officers jumped in their squad car and roared after the speeding car.

Poet's talked to his author in dreams about this, and Poet's convinced he was saved by the grace of good luck. The officers were bored and looking for a bit of malicious fun. Once the one policeman had finished ransacking his vehicle in search of drugs, and found none, Poet is sure they both would have roughed him up just for jollies, for something to do. Webster then and now is a relatively small town south of Houston. In the seventies the place was smaller and their police officers were hardly highly trained or supervised.

The other touch of evil—written about earlier in this book—concerns Poet's former brother-in-law from a previous marriage. The man was a Hell's Angels' type of biker, a Vietnam veteran, and a diagnosed paranoid schizophrenic on VA disability who had already murdered a man in Oklahoma, shooting him in the back of the head at a biker party. His biker brother-in-law Edward got off because no one would show up at court to testify against him. His motorcycle gang put out the word that if anyone showed up they'd be killed. Poet is quick to point out however that although Edward earlier had to shoot a man as an initiation to get into the biker club, he picked an old man to shoot in a drive-by on his Harley, and only shot the man, standing at a crosswalk, in the foot.

Poet's second wife was fond of her brother, and felt guilty for turning him into the police when he went AWOL from the army during the Vietnam War. The "brother" helped Poet and his then wife Courtney move from El Paso to Salt Lake City, hauling their belongings in his truck. Often this brother would tell his sister (Poet's wife) that he could kill her at any time, and her reply was always the same and simple, "I know that, Edward." Poet's brother-in-law—perhaps because of his war experiences—approached all human relations in terms of raw power. Edward let men know—if he felt more powerful than these men—that he could kill them or hurt them, not by direct speech, as he had done with Poet, but by tone of voice and body language. As you can readily imagine, the brother-in-law had few friends.

Poet felt his relationship with Edward was like being in a tiny totalitarian state. The brother-in-law always carried a blade in a leather case on his belt, and had pistols and rifles in his pickup. Poet's whole relationship with Edward was based on fear, but Poet felt compelled to put up with the biker on account of Courtney's love for her brother. All the unspoken faith and trust Poet had in others to behave decently—something he had assumed was natural and came with being alive—was wiped out. Poet had to constantly tiptoe around his brother-in-law for fear of enraging him, and a couple of times he did enrage him and large furniture objects got thrown around the room. Courtney was able to calm her brother down. For his own safety, Poet carried, hidden in his pocket on second key chain, a teargas spray he planned to use if things got too out of hand. After all, they had children in the house to protect.

These experiences have added to Poet's innate conservative upbringing. Though not wealthy, he has a great respect for order and peace. He sees these values as not natural to humans, but a thin veneer that can easily be swept away. Poet can only pray that parents all over the world continue to love their children, and bring them up with a sense of decency and respect for others. The hunger for power, the hunger for wealth and prestige, seems deep in the DNA. Only parental love, or perhaps the love of some other who cares for us when we are young, keeps us together. The author tells Poet in dreams that his mother was incapable of love, but he got love from his father when he was home from work, and from grandparents and an aunt, to whom he and his sister would be sent away during vacations, because his mother did not like taking care of children. The author whispers to Poet from the depths of sleep. *You speak of sadness and evil, Poet. You've told us twice here about the biker murderer. Now's the time to speak of graces that keep us sane and loving.*

Chuck Taylor

Life of a Poet

Poet suspects you'll be surprised and a bit disgusted when he tells you he woke early this morning and found in his bed a beagle, dead.

It was not the beagle of his childhood, Bugle Ann the family called her, come back from the dead, dead, though that would be have been a sight to see. No, this beagle's markings were different.

Poet may seem calm now, but he wasn't calm when it happened. Poet thought the mafia had gotten the wrong address, and left behind a warning for someone who'd gotten behind on payments for illegal drugs. But doesn't the mafia leave less expensive chicken heads?

Poet felt sorry for the beagle, and hoped he'd lived a good, long life. Poor puppy, poor dog. Poet hoped some angry critic who couldn't stand his verse had not killed the dog on his account. Poet felt like throwing up. He rushed into his small bathroom, but got control of himself and didn't lose his last night's supper.

With tears in his eyes, Poet buried the beagle in his small side backyard, reading passages from Ecclesiastes out of the Bible. "Nothing new under the sun," and "a time for this and a time for that." Sad to say, this was not the kind of thing where Poet could find as yet a snatch of meaning, even though that is his job as Poet.

Our artist packed up the family stuff in two hours, and they hit the highway in the station wagon for a remoter city west where rents were cheaper.

Even family poets travel light, and with the light.

Let's Be Reasonable

The great white sharks, Vampire notes, have of late been employed by twelve major metropolitan areas as firefighters and dogcatchers. The twentieth century was despicable in its treatment of members of the animal kingdom. Our new century has found uses for animals that make them economically viable while keeping them out of slaughterhouses and cans.

If used toilettes could be recycled instead of thrown in the dump—a hold over from the last, wasteful century—the money saved could relieve all the malnourished children in Terra Haute, Indiana. We need to collect all used Bic Lighters and glue them together, to build a border fence between Canada and the United States at least as tall as the fence along the Mexican line.

The art museums of this country should be emptied of their decadent paintings that could have been done by lovelorn elephants, and given over to any surviving Nazis worldwide to hide in caves. These museum spaces can be turned into repair shops for luxury automobiles and yachts. Music, because it attempts to replace God, should be listened to only when the populace is doing exercises, marching to war, or worshipping in churches.

Lion in Bed

Each night Poet puts his head inside a lion's mouth. His lion is insomnia. Poet carries a whip; Poet carries a chair. Poet knows of all his irresponsible wishes for happiness, and of all these tensions of his muscles keeping him awake for reasons he'll never comprehend.

Poet snaps the whip and gets insomnia up on the chair. Insomnia roars at him and swats with a sharp paw. Poet doesn't want me to put his head inside insomnia's mouth. Poet doesn't want to take in the smelly humid breath around his ears, but each night he must because he's got no other option. Poet's stuck in bed inside his fate.

Insomnia could snap down on Poet, though Poet's skilled at what he does. In goes his head; he tries to show no fear. Poet must, every night—if Poet truly loves life and wants to find some sleep on a free and lazy afternoon—never now fall asleep, not even for a moment, while in the lion's head.

Lion tells Poet not to worry. He has no grudges. Insomnia's his work and calling. "Just think of all the ideas you've had for poems with your head inside my mouth," says Lion. "Remember that novel you set in the Sereghetti? I think it's as good as Hemingway. Relish all the moments you can while waiting for the whispering tongue of death," Lion sighs in a half growl.

Choose Wisely

How much thought, Poet asks, in your no doubt busy days, have you given to the ceiling fans rotating over your head in public places? They have a steady cooling grace and silence, and some, hanging down below tin ceilings on poles, have been at their labors since the 1920's.

A ceiling fan in Salt Lake City's Lunt Motel kept Poet sane and cool through the early high fevered stages of Hepatitis B in 1976. She was an old one, right over poor Poet, as he lay in bed, but did her job smoothly and without complaint. Poet may owe his life to that ceiling fan.

Dust gathers on the blades, of course–life is just that way–and the blades deserve a cleaning to maintain their speed and grace, so they can continue to turn untiring. Poet has cleaned many a ceiling fan. Poet suggests that YOU ought to clean the blades on your ceiling fans.

Poet might have chosen the work as his paying profession, so as to better serve and do his duty. He might indeed have gone so far as to become a ceiling fan repairman, travelling from city to city. Such work has no doubt a humble moral dignity, could pay decently, and is badly needed.

Chuck Taylor

Poet once had a cheap modern ceiling fan crash down at the table next to him just missing his head, during a lunch of mushroom pizza while grading themes. Poet might have been a saver of lives, as a ceiling fan maintenance repairman. He's sad he didn't think of the idea sooner.

Vampire's Lost His Feet

Why would anyone raid his coffin and lop off his feet? Vampire thinks they stole his feet in Estonia—or perhaps in Lithuania or Latvia. Vampire wonders, why did he leave the new world to return to the old world? Why couldn't he have tolerated more Senator Ted Bruise, Michelle Botchman, and the Green Tea Party? With immortality, he doesn't really need Europe's universal health insurance. He came back, he figures, out of lonesomeness for the European landscape.

He needs to be more honest here. He's attempting to blame a superstitious peasant other, when it could be his lowly feet, enclosed in leather, got tired of being his feet and decided to take off. When was the last time Vampire took them dancing, got them a massage, or took them exploring a dark and narrow trail through the moors?

They could have been hungry for adventure, or wondered why Vampire lay about so often doing nothing to relieve his growing hunger. He could, at least on his off times, have attempted to save the baby seals from being clubbed to death.

Yes, his feet may have grown fed up. So many untried

directions of love and possibility and here Vampire remained, as if stuck in a nothing part of the world, with
barely enough coin to patch his cape, until the author
found him, and with a wave of the magic wand of his
pen, restored his feet and sent him back to the States.

Make Bones Strong

How many times have YOU had a gun flashed at your face? How many times have YOU come close to being blown away?

Poet walked through the wrong door at the wrong time and an Austin cop pulled a gun and raised it up to blast him from six feet away, and then the cop lost his fear. Poet figured the cop saw some gentleness and surprise in his face, and realized he carried no weapon beyond the breeze of his words.

The officer smiled a little and put his gun back in his holster. "Don't ever do that again," he said. "Don't ever come through a door when you're not expected."

Poet didn't say one word, but he wanted to ask, 'What the hell are you and your partner doing in the back of this convenience store? Looking for vampires? All I'm doing is bringing in the milk the little kids drink to make their bones strong.'

Chuck Taylor

Mercy, Mercy

Poet's known you long, and realizes that you are convinced you are a human being—one of the insect billions on this earthly ball—but Poet must be honest and tell you you're not human. Poet's sorry about dropping such a heavy ball on your toes, but there's nothing you or poet can do about it.

Please don't be disappointed. Things could be worse. Poet is here to inform you that you're a character in a fascinating if dark story written by a Russian author in the nineteenth century.

Poet can't say that the story has been made into a movie, or a video game, or that you've become a toy loved by many kids, but what the hell, it's only been a hundred and fifty years. Who knows what will happen? The important thing is that you are alive in the pages of a book.

Poet can't quite recall who the author is, or the name of the story. Maybe it will come to him, but Poet does recall that you are called Raskoinikov, in love with a gentle, long suffering woman, and that you have a better future ahead of you, with some rocky times of course. Poet's better at remembering stories than authors or titles.

The great advantage you have over biological humans is that you are immortal, or as immortal as anything can be. Paper is tough. It lasts a long time if it doesn't get wet, and let me tell you, you are in thousands of libraries all over the world, and you now speak many languages beyond your native Russian. OK, maybe one or two of the libraries have leaks in their ceilings, but that doesn't matter. You're everywhere, man, all at the same time, not like humans who are bogged down to one place at a time.

Poet is trying to do you a favor here. Why be limited to a story in one book? Poet is going to make you doubly alive, in two genres, already in the novel form and now in a tiny fiction. You'll be alive in this fiction but sadly or fortunately only the few but fit read such pieces. That might make you happy, and maybe even joyful. In this work, Poet is sending you down to Managua, Nicaragua—one of the poorest places in the world—and Poet's given you twenty thousand US dollars to play with, and you and your long suffering Sonia are going to give it all away. Your plane from Miami will land in Managua in five hours. The equatorial heat will offer an interesting contrast to the Siberian winters you experienced while in prison.

Sharp eyes you and your lovely lady have. Survey carefully the streets and give to those who are truly needy. You will probably decide to give to women dressed in old clothes with many children. Poet is setting this all up so you can make up for your mistake back in nineteenth century Russia. You deserve to be forgiven. You were a young man, a student too easily influenced by books, lonely, who did one terrible thing to a nasty, greedy woman who reminds us of today's Wall Street financiers. Poet, who also writes fiction, is providing you a means to do good and atone here in a proper Christian manner.

Poetry

Poet figures you might get it too, that swarm of red wasps blazing around in the brain. Poet's got a few friends, and sometimes when Poet looks at them, their heads will vibrate like crazed tuning forks, and then a few moments later their heads will look as if they could explode, like a pressure cooker without a steam release valve.

Some days, when the wasps get bad, Poet leaps in his pickup and drives far out of town into the Texas hill country, finds a remote stream off some gravel road, strips down, and lies in the cold spring waters, enjoying a benign sun overhead in the lonely blue. Time's slow passing brings him to a kind of calm.

Then poet thinks, you know, for all we know, what feels like wasps bursting from the skull could be a paradise of birds. They feel like wasps because you don't dare let them out around your human brothers, and you refuse to go fuzzy on prescribed medications.

It could be all these birds need to do is sing, in the special song of birds celebrating, until all their grief or joy gets released and can be offered to the stars like holy smoke.

Question

So where did they all go, those gals and guys that sat in a circle on wooden floors in rooms of old houses, never bogarting the joint, but passing it over and over to you and to you—but not to Vampire because Vampire was on the outside, didn't quite fit in? Ah Vampire walked by that room where friends gathered, smelled the weedy smell of the herb wafting and making him sneeze. It smelled so green, so grassy, but was not for him, since it filled his lungs with fluid and brought back his childhood allergies. If you didn't do the weed, you couldn't be in the circle.

Vampire also didn't wish to sit around because there was a lot of sky outside he hadn't seen, and also myriad leaves to meet in the sun and shake hands with.

So where did all these puffers go? They once were always around, though Vampire wasn't that close to them because he didn't imbibe. Are they stuck in the black uniforms of business now, stuck in rush hour traffic on a Austin freeway a couple of hours a day—at least the ones not dead? Vampire feels bad. Might they have bonded to form a lifetime palship, like the guys back from 'Nam, brothers forever? Perhaps they're all moved to Washington or Colorado, to puff in a golden cloud of freedom.

Sacagawea Dollars

Poet considers himself something of a physician, a doctor of the soul, put on the planet to heal, or at least serve as comfort in moments of craziness and trouble. All that goes without saying, but Poet wishes to say it anyway, in case you've forgotten, or you've not had the pleasure of meeting many poets.

You may not know that Poet is also your physical trainer. His job is to keep your psyche from becoming a couch potato, from developing a spiritual paunch. Some tough, resilient poetry's needed to develop survival muscles in the world that seems to like to spread shards of broken glass all over, often in hidden places. Poet, along with all the other poets, hopes to train you to be a firewalker– not the kind wearing asbestos shoes—but the kind who walks confidently across hot coals with feet in the nude.

But back to what was mentioned at the opening: physician of the soul. This Poet is now going to write a prescription in the form of a list of eleven reasons why you should be glad to be alive:

1) The whistle and rumble of freight trains in the middle of the night.

2) A tabby's meow of thanks when you open the door to let her in.

3) Snow magically gathering on the edges of wooden window frames surrounding small panes of wavy glass.

4) Carrot juice fresh out of the juicer.

5) Your dog's tongue flapping in the breeze with its head out the window.

6) Blazing yellow dandelions in the early spring yards of tolerant neighbors.

7) Sacagawea dollars tumbling out of the post office vending machine, change from buying stamps.

8) Fresh, free pecans gathered free off the streets of central Texas towns.

9) The sound of a great song blasting out of a hot convertible rocking at a traffic right next to your old Volkswagen.

10) Cornstalks rustling like a thousand leather jackets in an Iowa field.

11) An 'I love you' heart, with initials, carved into the trunk of a tall Colorado aspen.

You too can be a poet. Feel free to extend the list and share with others who seek some organic solace for the soul.

Stuck in What You Be?

I'm tired of sliding around invisible at night with my knife slitting so many throats, said the ninja warrior to the broad ornaments of stars, squating on the edge of a roof, exhausted from creeping around almost invisible in a creepy black suit, barely making a sound. Why shouldn't I be tired? This is post-war Japan! We know atomic bombs like no other nation!

I want to be like Beowulf or Gilgamesh or Achilles or like General McArthur with a corncob pipe, I want to roar from a cave and shoot dragon fire, but even more I want to go to baseball games and play cool video games. I want to drink cold cans of coke, but I don't want to be your friend, Vampire, even though you creep around in the dark dressed in black like I do.

So there.

Vampire, aren't you sick of the killing fields? Can't you go to a good dentist and unvampire yourself?

Maybe if I repeat my mantra over and over, you might alter as I have done: Baseball, video, cola; baseball, video, cola. It's the 21st century, man. Consumerism! What have

you bought lately? That's what they want of us. Why stay
obsolete?

The Blind of Lines

And you know all about lines, the lines to the left of you, the lines to the right of you, and here we are, stuck in the middle again, the black electrical wires above sure look like lines, the sidewalk has its sectional lines, the highway's got a dividing line down the middle, the Rock Island Line is a mighty good line, and then there's the thin blue line in prison for the guests of death row, as well as the red line you follow on the hospital floor that takes you to where they draw blood. Lines, the straighter the better we're told though the lines a river takes you on are crooked and this I'm telling you straight, Vampire says, and the rivers are older than we are and carry a crooked and ancient wisdom that says at times you don't want to travel a bee line, you want to twist this way and that, and then head back a ways, before channeling forward. What's the rush the river asks, the journey's as important as the destination. Now take my friend Jack over in Iraq, he was killed in the line of duty, though no one saw the line the bullet traveling from the rifle to his heart, and no one said where or where his line of duty began or ended, but everyone said he'd walked it, yeah he'd done it, a straight and narrow arrow hero, so line up boys, this just might be your turn.

Chuck Taylor

Part Three: "End"

There's No Such Thing

Poet is writing that the prose poem does not exist, even as you see the words appear before you on this sheet. When have you ever passed one on the street? When have you read one off an electronic billboard in Times Square?

Baudelaire's *Paris Spleen* does not exist.

Michael Benedikt's T*he Prose Poem: An International Anthology*, does not exist because it's out of print and always out of stock at stores.

Charles Simic's Pulitzer Prize poetry collection, *The World Doesn't End*, does not exist.

Everyone knows electronic music can't be real. All of us learned in high school that the electric starter could not be invented for the car, as was ably proven by the careful mathematical physics of the time.

The poem must rhyme at the end of the line and beat in a standard rhythm, so Walt Whitman doesn't exist. The poem needs lots of white space around it as a wall to fend off critics, and so poets can waste a lot of paper and fatten up the pages of their books.

The prose poem cannot be the nigger of literature. Niggers do not exist. Poet can't be that mystical beast the dragon. All that animal does is defeat armored knights in the pages of books, shoot out some fire, and fly away.

That's what you get for not existing. Everybody notices that you're not there, like the hole in the donut, like the empty space between faraway stars that's not, after all, so empty, it turns out...

To You, from the Demon in Your Head

Poet knows it astounds you—it astounds him—what grand shoehorns of stupidity humans are, and poet doesn't exclude myself from this sweeping generalization. Take brushing your teeth. Even in industrial nations, many let the food pile up and rot inside their mouths, loading the debris up and up through three meals at 98.6 F in a dark moist cave, not brushing till bedtime. Would you leave your hamburger meat out in the summer sun fifteen hours and then cook it to chow on down? Just think of the bacteria and germs feeding off the tiny stick 'ems of food in your mouth and on your teeth!

And how about wearing your shoes in the house, tracking in all that dirt and spit you've stepped in, and then getting down on the carpet to play with baby? Poet bets some of you put your purse down in the toilette stall where feet have tramped in every ten minutes, and maybe a little urine's dribbled down on the floor. A lot of stores, and lot of homes, don't swab their bathroom floors each and every day with Lysol. Poet bets you put your hands on shopping carts at the grocery store—or on doorknobs in buildings—filthy spots touched by who knows who carrying who knows what diseases, and then what do you do? You touch your hand to your mouth, dummy!

Poet bets tonight you're thinking of a long sweet kiss from the one you love. Have you thought of the teeth you'll meet when you go tongue slurping—the rotting food that's sitting in that mouth? "The mouth is home to billions of bacteria; in fact, the number of bacteria in the human mouth is similar to the number of people living on earth. Scientists have come across more than 700 different strains of bacteria in the human mouth, http://health-news.co.uk/how-dirty-is-your-mouth/. Leave the tongue slurping to the scandalous, French fry grease handlers.

It's a scallywag world out there. You know it. Poet knows it. Let me suggest you spend all your evenings cleaning your house, and that you carry disinfectant at all times to wipe your hands and to wipe any and all things you need to touch. Poet wants you to know Poet's on your side. People are always reaching out to shake your hand. You don't have to be that friendly. If that person has any intelligence at all, he or she will thank you.

You see, we are all of us on the stupid shoehorn side, but we are also angels from a higher plane out past the furthest asteroid belt. Our stay on this germy veil of tears is not for long. Should we not make it as pleasant as possible?

Chuck Taylor

Undressing

Suppose she were a poet so in love with her art that her words almost became the things themselves, that "the leaf" became green on a page, that the white of the page was moonlight, that the shadow of her hand on paper was blue—the sky itself. If she were that kind of poet and got confused she'd be spitting goat mad at the nerve of a US Poet Laureate undressing her, the now famous Emily Dickinson, on the page, yes mad even if she was pretty and pretty sure she dreamed many an evening of an undressing, in the blue shadows of a leafy night, under the milk of the moon, undressed by an imagined but real existing man, being assisted out of infinite Victorian stays and buttons of clothes, yes oh Lord on such wild nights! wild nights!

Mooring and mooring, so she couldn't hear the busy mortal buzzing of a fly nearby, but today she, now known all over the world and with a reputation to maintain, she'd would be so upset she'd get revenge, make, by force of arms, the US Laureate dress a naked guy in clothes, like a butler, in the sunlight of Italy, yes, because in grey drippy London to put on clothes in a poem with leafy hands would be illegal, certain jail time, but in the warmth of Italy all that would be needed would be a shadowed delicacy, a moonlight grace of touch to slide the trouser leg on the blue clubby foot of Byron, in the shake of the repulsed laureate's hands—Oh how he hates Lord Byron, and always has.

Chuck Taylor

The Seafood Restaurant

you inhabit spends its secret hours swimming under water. My restaurant –Poet doesn't know about yours—is a powerful Man of War jellyfish, many organisms tightly associated with each other to get the strenuous but necessary job done, just as in the day a restaurant is a cooperative organism of waiters, cooks, dishwashers, janitors, chefs, and so on. Do you love your seafood restaurant? A woman poet I know found her long lost twin sister there. A friend shared a secret that changed his buddy's life forever and for the better. Under water the seafood restaurant has a different sign hung out front. It is the smiling faces of the fish it kills, or has killed, to feed us above and make us happy.

Zoo Bar

An aardvark sashayed into a bar, an armadillo ambled
into a tavern and bumped into the barstool, a beaver beat
it to a saloon, a badger bopped into a public house, a cam-
el cruised in and kissed the counter, a cheetah crawled
in seeking prey, a dachshund danced panting into a bar,
a dingo dipped in joking up to the bar, a emu went into
a bar mooing, an earwig went into a bar without a wig,
a flamingo flew into a bar, a ferret ferreted into a bar, a
gorilla pounded his chest into a bar

a grouse groped into a bar,
a hammerhead shark swam into a bar,
a hyena laughed hilariously into a bar,
a iguana inched into a bar,
an ibis, trying to overcome shyness and low self esteem,
    inched into a bar,
a javelina jumped into a bar,
a Javan rhinoceros raced into a bar,
a killer whale proudly walked into a bar,
a koala bear cuddled cutely into a bar,
a lobster lollygagged into a bar,
a louse loafed into a bar trying not to louse things up,
a magpie moped into a bar,
a Maine coon crept into a bar,

Chuck Taylor

a newt never went into a bar,
a nightingale nervously nipped drinks in a bar,
an otter opened up an outrageous bar,
an orangutan operated the outrageous bar,
a partridge plunked into a bar

a peacock pounced into a bar carrying five golden rings
and a pear tree, and quail went into a bar, a quoll from
Australia went into a bar—a Chicago bar on Polk Street
Poet's always promoting—a roseate spoonbill rocked in,
a rock hopper penguin hopped in, then a Saint Bernard
and a Siamese fighting fish, a toucan tiptoed in, then in
trotted a Tasmanian devil, a viper vamoosed into the bar,
and a vulture vaulted in smelling beef jerky, a weasel
and a wallaby walked in real palsy-walsy, an X-ray tetra
traipsed in all alone, then a yak followed by a Yorkshire
terrier, and then a Zebra, and finally at last a zorse.

When the bartender saw the zorse he couldn't believe his
eyes, and then when the zorse told him he was a zorse the
bartender didn't believe his ears. The bartender checked
the Internet on his cell phone to see if the animal existed.
He was amazed to find actual photographs. It was not at
all a fantasy animal like a unicorn or griffin. The bartender, a humorless man with a walrus mustache who didn't
like animals put down by bad jokes, as a rule did not
serve drinks to fantasy animals, but he was pleased today
and made an exception. No one was fighting; no animal
was eating another. Everyone seemed to want to party.
The bartender called up Poet for advice. Poet suggested
he change his name to Adam and to rename the saloon
The Eden Bar. The bartender ordered drinks on the house
for all around—even for the dragon hanging his head in
the corner, studying the tunes on the jukebox.

God, a busy deity these days, dropped by to say hello and

reminisce about the Old Testament days when he some-times spoke to people, but didn't stay long. Putting out a hand and smiling, God passed on all the generous and friendly offers of drinks.

God, it turns out, worships himself these days as a Southern Baptist.

Chuck Taylor

Salvation

Have you ever had a goat spit in your face? Vampire has, and luckily Vampire got the message. That was long ago, before the zoo people added glass to protect the gapers.

No creature wishes to be caged and gawked at by some other creature. Spitting goats are not cuddly Teddy bears to warm us under our covers.

They may feel you've come to eat them, and if we wished to treat goats with dignity, we'd hunt them over tall rocky mountains and through thick brush; we'd take our shot, and if we killed a goat, we'd thank our gods and the goat for the blessing of food to feed our families, then carry the meat back to the village.

But no, something in our DNA gives us a thrill to control and dominate. It's the show of shows, to control, to dominate, to torture and maim, and maybe to kill. We're imperialists of our home, this planet—after the minerals in the soil, after the treasures of the seas, after the winds themselves, the mouth open and ready to devour all the way up to the moon and planets . O how we busy ourselves with the constant planting of flags.

OK. Go ahead, it's fine to feel disgust with your own kind. That's a spiritual beginning. Whitman said we must work out our own salvation.

Art

Vampire knew a man who trained a Peppered moth to sit where his shirt buttoned at the neck, in order to make a living bowtie, a bowtie exceeding the beauty of anything made by human hands. The man kept a cotton swab dipped in sugar water pinned just behind the top button on his shirt so the moth could feed.

Most people feel slightly uneasy about staring for long at a man's neck with a bowtie, so few made the leap of imagination to see that what was actually before them—the world's only living bowtie—and no one dared risk appearing stupid by asking, "So is that an icky moth you've got sitting there at your throat?"

The moth was marvelously and mesmerizingly patterned—far beyond what any textile manufacturer could pull off—and slightly fuzzy, so it looked like a warm and fuzzy fabric beyond any fabric known to man.

The moth could remain still for hours and was quite pleased with itself, pulling off such a grand deception.

The Bright Abstracts

You know how it is. You're sitting around, staring at the bright abstracts on the hospital walls, and waiting to hear, after you've had your CAT scan, if your cancer has come back.

Cancer is so silent. It never shares a word with you, but your dog might be able smell it.

You asked your doctor how you got the cancer and he said, "Oh Poet, don't know, maybe gamma rays."

You tell your doctor that perhaps some kinds of cancer result from the bite of a vampire that comes in your window and tastes your neck in the middle of the night. He offers a wan smile but doesn't laugh.

For thousands of years the brightest theological and philosophical minds, mostly men, have scribbled their hearts out, deep into the night, trying to prove that life's more than a roll of bone-colored dice.

She

In the description of male vampires, no one has pointed out how much these highly romantic nineteenth century creatures are dedicated to roses, or how they tend so tenderly these flowers in collapsing old greenhouses, down old neglected trails deep in the woods of their forgotten Transylvanian estates.

It is not hard to see why, like that other outcast, Shakespeare's Moor Othello, they treasure these highly symbolic flowers, especially today the hardy American Beauty variety.

They appreciate their wide petals, so close to the color of blood, and so soft and tender, like passionate young flesh.

They appreciate the nuanced shadings of the petals' red, suggesting such strong and varying emotions.

The perfume of the flower is so much like the anticipated beloved's exhaling breath. Their thorns, so much like Vampire's own bicuspid fangs. No one complains of the roses' thorns.

A female vampire with any modicum of romantic taste dare not enter a greenhouse full of roses on a full moon night. Don't ask me why, but she will run screaming out of the place, on the verge of tears and madness.

Penguins

Then there came a day when the woman Poet hated him so much Poet tried mouthing out loud all her ideas, as a way to bring HER back at least inside his soul. If Poet could keep HER voice and thoughts inside his head SHE would like him and never leave.

Poet was far from HER. SHE'S in Dallas working in a downtown and living on the poor end of Italian Avenue, taking care of three children. Poet had found himself in an Austin room of total strangers, feeling alone and abandoned, searching for some relief in this group of folk musicians and their road friends.

The woman that Poet loved spoke out of *his* head HER ancient idea–perhaps a truth, perhaps not—but not heard much in the 2000s. "Birds were given wings to fly; women were given uteruses to make babies."

The woman folksters had their guitars out and were plucking tunes. It didn't show on Poet's face how his soul was all mangled bloody muscle. The folk group was into their Bohemian lives, traveling in old cars, often sleeping out on some country road till they reached the city of their next engagement, where they'd give, for next to no money, the blessings of their songs.

The Kerrville Folk Festival outside Austin was beginning in a few days. One of the woman folk singers finally spoke up as Poet droned on, spoke up by strumming her guitar and singing, "What about penguins? O, O, what about penguins? Are the females no longer females because they don't fly with their wings?"

Poet was not at all irritated by her disagreement. The pain in his self cooled a bit. Perhaps all he needed to do was blab and blab, like her schizophrenic brother Edward did when medicated, to get all HER voices out of his system.

Agree

In all his years Vampire had never known a woman who hated her father as much as Gloria did. Her blood was bitter; he could smell it.

Gloria's father had inherited a large farm of dark topsoil in the bend of the Brazos in Texas. When he reached his fifties his joints began to ache from the heavy labor of running the operation, so he sold the place against the wishes of his wife, who did not wish to move away from her grown daughter and friends.

Estes and Alsace divorced, and he took off for Mexico. Alsace got half the proceeds and bought a house in Bryan, with enough cash left over, it seems, that she never had to take a job. Her daughter Gloria also divorced her trucker husband, who was rarely home, and took a job in Korea teaching ESL.

Once in Mexico, father Estes settled in the small, former silver mining town, Real de Catorce, high in the mountains. In a year he was married to a local woman twenty years younger, in her thirties, and began to learn Spanish. Eventually they had two children.

Chuck Taylor

Vampire was a more an acquaintance than a friend with the woman with the bad blood in her family. Alsace refused to speak of her farmer husband. Perhaps it was not working and having little to do that made her pass away on the young side, in her early sixties. Vampire had heard she liked the sauce a lot.

When Gloria told him the story on returning home for her mother's funeral, to explain why she refused to see her father Estes or even invite him to the event, Vampire—out of a certain old world courtesy—pretended to sympathize and agree.

Irresistible

Along with having a special organ to draw blood out of its victims, and a tube to feed the blood into the digestive system, the vampire is almost absent of intestines because his system is dealing with a liquid rich in nutrients easily absorbed, not chewed solid food that must be broken down by acidic acids and intestinal fauna and flora symbiotic in humans and absolutely necessary for successful digestion.

Rarely do you spot an overweight vampire because they eat so little and their digestive equipment is so limited. It is also why vampires are so gorgeous. With hardly any intestines, their bellies are flat, their abs rock hard six-packs, and in contrast to most human males the male vampires seem to possess powerful chests, and the women vampires possess ample bosoms.

No wonder they are, unlike Poet, irresistible.

Life is Full of Trouble

Poet can't sit down in his own home because the two Siamese fight to sit on his head. They don't bother his wife. They don't bother his children. Perhaps they're trying to make Poet as royal as themselves, to crown him king of the household castle, and will fight each other for the honor.

Poet'll toss them half across the room, but they always come back. Poet'll put them in the bedroom but they'll paw the door open. Two Siamese, fighting for position at the top of his head – it's just too bizarre.

Poet has nice hair, true, and the view from up on top is good. Poet is like a tree with moving arms that can drive away any potential predators, or perhaps the Siamese are predators. Perhaps they're eyeing the jugular in his neck, dreaming themselves vampires, or about to transform into vampires.

They are waiting, waiting, the patient way cats are able to wait, for the exact moment to pounce.

On Love

You know how miserable you get when you are not in love. You know how crazy and immobile you become when your love is gone for a week, but then you know also the weight of love, how you wear the heavy thing like a flax jacket at all times for protection against the knives of words or glances that get tossed around in the battle for power. Oh the jockeying for position, the struggle of making everyday momentous, life-changing decisions!

You identify with Plastic Man who can bend to meet any need or compromise, and you're also attracted to the quickies by the window of Vampire.

Vampire is in and out. He gets the sustenance he needs and is so satisfied he has no need to claim ownership, to drag the loved one to the lock tree of marriage. He just flies away.

What did you say? Are you talking to me?

Never mind. You're not listening.

There are days you fly away too.

Dollar

Vampire knows you've noticed how shopping has re-placed religion. In his state they used to try to stop it by keeping the stores closed Sunday mornings, and then by limiting what could be sold, but the big wigs won that battle. Vampire goes to the dollar store and wonders if it's such a bad thing that they're Sunday open.

Everyone gets to pick her or his own household god, buy it and take it home. That's freedom of religion for you; that's true diversity of faith. The shoppers at the dollar store are tense with joy and expectation. Everything's just a dollar! They don't have to say much to each other as they search for meaning up and down the aisles.

Even the hated poor can find a dollar to spend and can feel a part of the congregation. Vampire bought a cane made in China with a glass eye to beat off dogs that attack him, for a dollar! Careless owners let them run at night unleashed in our city's large, wooded parks.

Vampires are on the back wall, in the toy section, plastic toys for boys made in Indonesia.

Useless Speculation

Poet gets tired of looking at the world through a man's eyes and wishes to have the eye of the turtle, or the eye of the cat, or the eye of the human woman who walks with the danger of a baby dropping out between her legs, at least until menopause. Most women seem to want babies to drop out of them, even though it's painful and some risk to their own heath and lives; some even seem to want more than one. Still, these women take an interest in other things, and many follow those interests to remarkable accomplishments, like Doris Kearns Goodwin, who writes presidential biographies.

Women don't seem to get smothered in metaphysical whining. Maybe it's the beards that get men into moldering around in the brain, as they finger their chin hairs. Almost all men who could wore beards up until the coming of the 20th century and the modern safety razor. A lot of moldering was done before then. Perhaps women get too wrapped up in both their chosen work and childcare to worry about the boulder being rolled up the hill that always rolls back down on the dark nights of Camus absurdity, or to worry that we all die and come to nothing, less than microscopic dust, compared to a immense expanding universe.

Chuck Taylor

Somehow, Poet can't imagine the dark philosophers Schopenhauer or Nietzsche as women. Perhaps it's the smell of baking bread, the cheer of cutting crisp vegetables, or the laughter in the kitchen, far from the outside world of competition where all is made to seem small, that keeps women on an even, miraculous keel. Poet's only a man, but he's been fortunate to feed plenty of babies with an astonished heart. Looking down at the baby's face, Poet didn't think once about the whirling meaninglessness of existence. How could he with so many sparklers in the baby's eyes?

Usually it was dark and very late. Usually Poet was exhausted, wakened by a four AM feeding, but Poet was joyous, always.

Dinner Together

Somehow Vampire and Poet ended up sitting across from each other, years ago, at a table in Berghoff's Restaurant in Chicago.

"You're no better than I," Vampire said. "I know exactly what you do." He took an elegant sip of his Chardonnay

"And I know what you do," said Poet, "or what you do mythologically."

"You're the one who sucks blood. You steal people's stories. You steal the blood of their lives and emotions. You squish it down on the cold page for strangers to see. It's all meat through the sausage maker, Poet. You don't give a cracked crock for a single person that you descriptively devastate."

"I'm a storyteller, Vampire. I bring in the miracle of light, the healing power of stories to evaporate the dark demons inside. I create symphonies out of words."

"It's healing to embarrass people? When will you post your first YouTube to cause a suicide?"

"A lot of stuff I make up. I create composite characters. I change hair colors and locations, and yes, stories do heal people. The stories and their music can dissipate the pain that seems forever stomped in the back cells of the brain."

"Well, I'm not so heroic. Mine's a more humble path. I'm just trying to survive. I can't buy what I eat at Safeway."

"Why the quarreling?" Said Poet. He lifted his glass of wine and saluted the creature sitting across the table. "Where would literature be without vampires and all that you stand for? The white gloves, the black suit, the cape. Death has never been so beautiful, so aesthetic, so sexy!"

"Check please," said Vampire. "It's getting late and I have work to do. We'll meet another time, I am sure—and I'll tell you my tales."

That Would Be Nice

Vampire had been chased by alligators before, out in East Texas, and since Vampire can fly, he thought alligators would wind fast and he'd leave them far behind. But it does take Vampire a while as a seven hundred year old to get up speed and lift off earth, like any big old swan. Vampire figured alligators didn't like getting too far from water, but these two full adult males kept coming as Vampire dodged between small pine trees.

Vampire swore one had an alarm clock inside going tick-tock like in *Peter Pan*. He could imagine nothing more gruesome than to be torn apart by alligators fighting over his body at supper, so when he spotted a tree—a tall hardwood—that he could leap up high enough to grab a low branch and drag himself up, that's what he did.

The alligators did not give up, even though the branch was too high for them to grab with their mouths. They started trying to chomp through the trunk of the tree to bring it down. Vampire started breaking off branches that were dead and flinging them as best he could like spears.

He climbed higher and looked for a place between two branches where he could lodge his body and maybe sleep

Chuck Taylor

through the day. Certainly the alligators would be gone by morning. Didn't he have enough to worry about with Poet around always moaning? Vampire heard a plane overhead, so he climbed as high as he could and waved his cape as a flag.

You're Vampire, you know, he thought as he waved his cape at the distant speck in the sky that he hoped wasn't an airborne Buffy, the slayer. You're supposed to be aware of the darkness of things. What is the meaning of this? Hey, wait a minute, do you suppose you're dreaming the whole thing? Life, they say, is a dream, and you could shake yourself awake, but are you really in a coffin dreaming? If not, shaking could cause you to come crashing down out of this tree.

Vampires and Poets

Everything Vampire stands for, the modern Poet stands for the opposite. The Vampire never needs to cook; Poet tries to fix gourmet meals every evening for his honey.

The Vampire's decisive in love—at least he was before feminism. Is he confused now? Poet wrings his hands in the sweat of love and squeezes out sonnets.

Poet works to save the rainforests; Vampire grows hothouse roses and enjoys his buddy Crow.

Vampires are relatively rare; Poets swim the streets of everywhere in out of style Goodwill outfits.

Vampires like to work the dark of night, solitary. Once satisfied, they return to their narrow wooden beds. Poets gather in a room with many sofas, where they jump up and down like monkeys on cushions, squawking poems whose subtext often seems to proclaim, "Look at me! Look at me!"

Chuck Taylor

Vampire Women

The notion does not come solely from his own experience, where woman have remained Goddesses, but from the experiences also of his friends and family. Thus Poet has learned that some women, as well as men, can be vampires.

Now it's come to seem to him that some women vampires have another way of working—less flamboyant perhaps, but more clever and subtle.

Take Poet's mother. She never worked a job a day in her life, but she worked the credit of his father. The law was always pounding on the door, trying to serve warrants. Dad had installed inside locks on all the castle doors so the kids wouldn't forget, open the door, and let the law in. The castle was piled high, mostly with expensive brand name clothes, furniture, and jewelry in every room. We made our way around the place down narrow paths.

Poet's best friend's two wives, one after another, never wanted children. They didn't work, they didn't have children, and the best friend, who managed a restaurant, did the cooking after work. Maybe the wives did the laundry, but mostly they read books, both of them, the same combination of romance novels and feminist theory, checked out from the branch library. The books were piled up everywhere that the dishes weren't piled up—on the floor, on the chairs and table and dressers.

Women don't have to go to school to become mythical vampires. They know how to suck the blood, in the coin of any realm, indirectly. This form of vampirism seems accepted behavior in numerous cultures. Of course not all women remain satisfied. Though perhaps dependent at first on a man's salary, many seem determined to grow wings and hunt of their own.

Valentine's

Back in the day, and Poet's talking of the late forties and fifties, it wasn't required on Valentine's Day that every kid give in class every other kid a Valentine. The children were allowed more freedom, allowed to develop their own judgment, and choose whom they wanted to valentine, and whom they didn't. It worked like adult life. The popular girls and boys got piles of Valentines that filled up the tops of their desks, and some of us—maybe one of you—got two or three, one from the teacher.

As the grades at school progressed, we got used to it, but that didn't mean it didn't hurt, that we did not dream to be out in the night, flying around the neighborhood for that feeding moment of love, and then to sleep perhaps in our beds alone, in the solace of silence, done till we hungered again.

Love Letter to the 60's

Poet's pissed because he's not a sorcerer. Poet never stood in a sorcerer's shadow. He never even saw slink a sorcerer's shadow up a wall.

Do you have any idea what is was like to learn that Uri Geller could not move a glass of water with his fierce gaze, or bend a half dollar?

The Bard walked through deserts beyond deserts, high-rise office buildings of deserts, shopping malls of deserts. He boiled creosote under a wolf moon in an iron pot over an open fire and drank the stinking juice and threw up. After par boiling off the thorns, poet fried up slices of prickly pear and ate it seasoned with jalapenos. Did he see the green god? Did he see the rising sun of Godzilla? God himself knew how badly Poet needed to fly. The need ran through all the molecules of who he was. Poet stepped off a ten-foot ledge expecting to saunter through air and fell on his ass.

What a frickin' fuckin' liar you were, Carlos Castaneda, and you knew you were the world's widest liar. That's why you hid under the brim of your hat and had no friends. That's why you died without telling anybody, and set up a cult of only women members, led by yourself.

Poet's neighbor, teenage son of the town druggist, got hooked on morphine by stealing the key to the drug box, all because of you and your chronological confusions of best-selling scribblings. His mother and father had to send him to a fundamentalist Christian camp to get him off the drug, and the boy ended up writing long letters his parents telling them what sinners they were.

A lava lamp, these days, is sorcery enough for Poet, thank you.

Thank You, Percy Shelly

Sometimes the Bard wants to be Shelly and fall upon the thorns of life. He wants his pants torn and toes cut, and he wants to shout "I bleed!, I bleed!"

Poet could then head home, take a shower, put Mercurochrome on his cuts, and slip into a new more stylish pair of pants.

But what do you do when you don't even get a chance to fall on the thorns of life? What do you do when life is an attack dog, or a drone crashing out of the sky at your face?

Yes, these days life lunges, like a car out of control at full speed, with sharp metal grill-teeth. This is hard on Poet, and hard on everyone. These words are being scanned at the NSA as they're typed.

Since life can stun, it's good to carry a stun gun in your pocket. They make them disguised as cell phones and small flashlights.

Take control of your life. Don't go out much. Live deep in a cave high in the mountains, and when you do go out, carry the stun gun. Stand in the shadows of life and hope the hounds go sniffing under the wrong bushes.

At least then you can feel more in charge, for a while.

Breaking the Staff

They always want Poet to stop making sense, like the pitted green olives in the tall glass jars forming a choir on the moon to sing to the craters. The trouble is, Poet was a marine once, and could pull himself up the rope ladder in basic training till the muscles in his body were true obedient slaves, but these monkeys have grown lax and yet they remain here, whole colonies, like red ant mounds in his backyard. They live under his shirt and in his underpants, each little stigmata bite telling Poet also to stop making sense.

People are tired. No one listens, they say, and it's reached the point where language wants its freedom from meaning if not grammar. So what if you were like Prospero out of Shakespeare once with a white magic staff that could by words command? Ariel, his word's invention, wants her freedom too.

It's getting so Poet can't even describe an adobe wall crumbling in the desert west of El Paso. The emotions of stars, hippos, hippies, horses—all beyond Poet's powers—but you, muse, whoever you are, whip Poet with the universal tongue and make Poet go on and on like he were picking cotton under a nail-driving sun. His bastard tongue never seems to feel exhaustion.

And why all the reasons, the explanations, the excuses, the suffering? Ariel whispers at Poet. You're no better than Prospero. Why lay that on my poor airy back? Let me free far from your bars of rules to stop making sense, let me flit and flip around in the tempests of the wind free as an ozone molecule, like spinning pizza dough tossed in the air at Papa John's. Ideas, colorless and green. Then I, Ariel, will be able to sleep furiously.

Battle of the Poems

Poet tells the story of when a bunch of buddy prose poems got off the school bus at the usual stop, but were astounded to find themselves suddenly surrounded by lined poems, most of them long poems with hefty hexameter arms.

A language poem issued a sentence that contained seven exclamation marks but no one knew exactly what the sentence meant—or what to do.

A nature poem suggested the prose poems be banished to the forest, to be used by the witch of the woods in her new recipe for a water impermeable gingerbread house.

A Bukowski poem burped and said the easiest thing to do would be to drink the prose poems under the table and prove they were not men.

The Vampire poems hung back. They didn't care who won the battle. They only wished to sample the blood of whichever brood of poems lay wounded and defeated.

The confessional poems said tell us your secret intimate sins and then kill yourselves.

The fight finally began. The prose poems were far out-numbered and it looked as though they'd be crushed like autumn leaves caught in a mower and hauled away in plastic bags.

But then a Whitman poem, bearded and lusty, stepped out of a gym from across the street. He blew the other poems over like playing cards with an operatic breath the likes of Paul Bunyan bragging.

"You too I embrace, prose poems, as I embrace the clown behind the horse in the circus parade shoveling up the horseshit, as I embrace the catatonic teenage boy who spends his life in his rooms with Skittles and computer video games. Come ride with me the windy Brooklyn Ferry. You are done with your pathetic plastic years in the schooling of buses. I am your wound dresser and will wash your feet, as a humble act of honor, as did my bud-dy Jesus back in Judea days."

The Whitman poem tipped its hat. "You have obeyed lit-tle, and resisted much."

Poet in Residence, Vampire University

It was a long ride, mostly by bus, at times by flat bottom boat, deep into the bayous of Southern Louisiana for the young MFA Poet, recently graduated from a program in El Paso, to visit the rather obscure campus of Vampire University, deep in the swamps, her third job interview this year. Last year she'd been to six campus interviews and failed to find a position.

It was a bad time for MFA poets. The economy had turned into a rotten apple, universities had mostly stopped hiring, and many of her friends had gone into advertising, following in the footsteps of the famous beat poet Lou Welch, who wrote "Raid Kills Bugs Dead."

To be frank, the Chairman of the English Department said, as Poet sat down at a chair in front of his desk, your grades were good but not sterling, and your letters of recommendation were enthusiastic but did not speak of brilliance. What caught our attention were the batch of sample poems you sent, and their use of blood imagery. It made the committee think of D.H. Lawrence and Robinson Jeffers. Would you care to elaborate on your use of such imagery, or symbolism?"

"Blood is such a powerful word," said the young MFA Poet. "It carries so many deep associations, both of life and death. As a woman I must deal with blood every month."

"We noticed you sometimes write of 'bad blood.' " In your estimation, as a creative artist, is there such a thing as bad blood? Might people be harmed by ingesting—accidentally of course—bad blood?" We here have a great respect for the insights of creative artists.

"It's a bit of a Victorian word," said the writer, "but still powerful. Mental illness runs in families—people have long noticed—and the idea existed that the illness was passed on down through the blood."

"So you see it more as a metaphor?"

The young MFA was growing uncomfortable. "Yes and no," she said. "I have mental illness in my family—my uncle, my father, my brother. It seems to travel the fraternal line. One could say there's something wrong in the DNA, but then how does the illness reach into every remote cell of a body. Only the blood touches every cell of the body. And why does it touch only the males?"

"So you think that if someone were to actually drink this 'bad blood'—I say again by accident of course—they could become mentally ill themselves?"

"I can't rule it out," said the poet. "Medical science remains in its infancy. A lot remains to be learned."

"We are prepared to offer you a one year appointment," said the chairman, "with a two-two teaching load. Your pay at the Assistant Professor level will start at fifty thousand. How does that sound? The only stipulation would be that you'd need to work closely with a biologist on our campus on further research into 'bad blood.' Will that work for you?"

The young MFA poet thought a moment. Did she want to go back to making donuts at Shipley's in El Paso? She'd been around enough universities to know that they were full of bad blood, and had grown used to it over the six years she'd spent in higher education. Something had to be done about her sixty thousand dollar school debts.

"I accept," the young woman said. "By the way, how in the world did you ever get the name of Vampire University?"

'Our wealthy founder back in 1876," the chairman said. "Without his endowment we could not continue to exist. Sadly he had a sense of humor that was a bit twisted, and he dabbled in New Orleans voodoo."

Warped

Vampire's warped, but how he got that way, and when, he cannot tell for certain. Was it seeing his first preying mantis on the windowsill climbing the castle stairs? Was it the wide splay of stars that outlined for him the enormity of the blackened universe above, having only pinpricks of light scattered around? Vampire was oddly consoled. He'd have plenty of darkness to move around in.

It could be Vampire's brain grew warped or it could be his personality, bent over inside like a crabbed hunchback. His spine could be warped from the heavy weight of himself that he carries. Time is warped and moves at warp speed. Night after night, ladybugs hatch to do their thing somewhere on the planet, yet it seems he moves more slowly and has more grey hair, and that is unseemly for a person of his profession.

When Vampire goes pub-crawling, it's not victims he is seeking. Vampire is looking for the other warped, as announcers talk about finding Jesus all over the radio. Be they no street killers though, and be they no serial drinkers. Vampire's the only killer he wants to know.

Never admit you're warped—Vampire knows that

much—it chases the lovely ladies away he might consider drinking from. One day he knows he'll make it into the warp and weave, or is it the warp and woof. Then he knows there will be gods who are envious.

The Kind of Night It Was

"I'm the rational type and while my female friends are always seeing a horny guy ghost down in the basement of our bookstore, I go down there all the time and never see anything but work to be done," says Poet. "I also go down there to catch a nap."

Poet feels a bit deprived. Who wouldn't mind a haunting in their lives every now and then to zest up life?

Finally, at three in the morning, an apparition appeared — not at work — but at the foot of the bed back in his apartment. It's aspect seemed kindly, but just to be sure Poet pulled the pistol out from under his pillow and asked the white ghostly thing if he — or she — could be some kind of vampire.

"I know you always wondered why I'd have nothing to do with you when I was alive," the ghost said.

"Is that you, mom?" Poet was sure he recognized the voice. "You bet I was aware of your distance, at least subconsciously as a kid, but I had little basis for comparison. I thought all mothers were that way and never gave it much thought. How are you doing in the other world, ma?"

"Troubled, son. Troubled. I wasn't much of a mother. I'd never even played games with you or your sister. Remember me always saying, 'I'm not your social chairman.'"

"I remember that, mom. I'd forgotten it till you mentioned it. You just didn't like kids—any kids. You told my sister Laney and I that all the time. You said you'd wished we'd never been born and it was dad who made you do it. They're not torturing you or anything, are they mom? If they're giving you a hard time, I'd be glad to write you a letter of recommendation."

"A letter. I don't know if it would do me much good where I am."

"I'll get some inflammable paper. Mom, you taught me how to love the lonely. Remember how when I was sick with asthma at five and six and you'd almost never came in my room? Dad had to bathe me. That was a true trial by fire, mom. It was so hard to get air in my lungs and I never knew if I'd live through the night. Boy you sure taught me to be strong. You were tough love before there was tough love."

"But what about me? Who was I to talk to when your father became a drunk and you and your sister left home for college?"

"I figured that's why you took all those sleeping pills and killed yourself, mom. You were being smart. You got yourself out of a bad situation. But say, it must be fun to be a ghost. You can go where you want whenever you want. You don't have to worry about rent or feeding yourself. I bet you've tons of friends now. Do you use Facebook?

You could form the "Reluctant Mothers' Club" and commiserate with other such moms. Do a little group therapy. Maybe you suffered from post-partum depression all those mom years."

"Are there vampires where you are? I'd keep my distance from them, if I were you. Is there a way you can introduce me to the ghost in your bookstore basement?"

Do as Humans Do

Vampire often looks at human culture like an anthropologist. He is on the outside and likes to attempt scientific objectivity, and he must sadly admit that he's picked up on numerous human cultural flaws.

For one, it's a mistake that children learn so early that they must die. The fact of death creates too much anxiety and too many horrid and narrow religious excuses.

Vampire holds that a few lies should be told by those that know to those who are ignorant, to preserve all children's innocent happy smiles as long as possible. One lie should be like the story of storks flying around delivering babies, holding white bundles of joy in their beaks. Another lie could be the Santa Claus story.

The bodies of the dead should be disposed of secretly by a squad of ninja knowers, and then the innocents can simply told that the dead have gone on a long vacation, up to the North Pole, to assist in making toys for Santa's workshop. If that won't work, the innocents can be told that the adult has to take a job in New Zealand, too far away to come home often.

And, Vampire points out, those poor little elves up in Santa land tire quickly and could use some help, even if the help is only imaginary. Indeed, the elves despair of the huge task of making toys for every child on the globe, and would love to hear that dead people have volunteered to help. It's about time, the elves think, that the humans provide some payback to show they're grateful for the incredible work the elves have done it seems like forever.

Vampire suggests that the lies include a smaller lie: that vampires transport the rarely vacationing North Pole or New Zealand dead humans like Eagles carrying their prey in talons. Children would then grow up with a better opinion of vampires.

Also, Vampire has known the elves a long time, since both creatures share in common the trait of immortality. He is well aware of how the elves despair of their enormous Christmas task, and often wish they could do as humans do, and die.

Identity

They were working for Manpower in Dallas back in the 70's, about fifteen of them, unloading furniture in the sweltering August heat, carrying it into the forty rooms of a new La Quinta Inn on Central Expressway.

Lisbeth was the only woman on the team. The foreman was desperate, and took her on because she was six foot two. Lisbeth needed to get some dollars together to finish the book she was writing. The guy she worked with had just graduated from a divinity school in Dallas somewhere. Kenneth was a hard worker, but he couldn't keep his mouth shut.

As the two carried the furniture inside the room and assembled it, he keep pushing and pushing, trying to convert her.

"You know," he said, "unless you accept Jesus, and are baptized into the full faith and name of the Lord, you will go to hell."

"That's nice," Lisbeth answered, wiping the sweat from her forehead with her arm.

"No, hell is not a nice place. I think you know that." The boy had intense blue eyes and short dirty blond hair.

"I can tell you with good authority," Lisbeth smiled back, "there is no long-term hell, only short-term hells like we're in now."

Kenneth looked back at her with an expression of both shock and incomprehensibility. Her words shut him up for the rest of the day.

The next day, a Tuesday, Kenneth picked up with his obsession. "You realize, don't you, that you can do good works until the cows come home, but those good works won't get you to God unless you're baptized in the Lord."

"I don't do good works," Lisbeth came back. "I am, as an artist, too selfish. Listen, Kenneth, I understand you're a new greenhorn graduate. All you do is make assertions. I could assert the sky is polka dot. Why don't you leave me alone and let's do our work as best we can?"

"You're soul is more important than any stupid job," Kenneth countered.

"If you don't shut up I'm going to tell the boss and go work with another."

On Wednesday Kenneth tried another tack. When Lisbeth thought about it later she considered maybe it was some technique he'd learned in divinity school. You throw a person off balance by insulting them and then you can get inside and convert them.

"I gather your man is quite a player," Kenneth said out of the blue, as they carried a mattress into a second floor room.

"We're both players," Lisbeth shot back, "trying to turn the insult into a joke. "We play on the same softball team."

"No," I mean, "he was married two times before, right? And you're not married. That makes you a whore, you know, living in sin."

The young man was on the carpet looking up at her. She despised the smart-ass, jaunty self-assuredness that only a person a twenty-five could have, convinced he had all of life figured out. Kenneth looked down to put a wheel on the bed frame, and while he was looking down, Lisbeth grabbed a lamp that was still without its shade and hit him hard on the head with its base.

She got on her knees, pulled his head into position, and bit into the jugular of his neck. She drained enough blood out of him to make him weak but not to kill him. Then she pressed her fingers down on the fang marks for a number of minutes to staunch the bleeding.

Lisbeth stood up and wiped her mouth with her right arm, muttering an "Ah!" of satisfaction, as if finishing a warm and delicious bowl of tomato soup. She rolled down her shirtsleeves on both her arms and buttoned them at the wrist. Now any spots of blood on her right arm were covered.

"Well, I'll have to work up another identity again," she thought, as she walked down the stairs and off the job site. "I think I'll do my hair red, and I'll do my nails up long and fancy. A secretary's sit-down job, just temporary—that's what I want, because it's always hard for a vampire to work during the day. We're batty night creatures. "

His So Far Lucky Life

Your parents, your teachers, your coaches, and even your minister—they all say the same thing: Do the best that you can. No one ever says how exhausting it is to be always at your best—or how stressful.

Vampire works to make extra income as a magician. Vampire tries to pull rabbits out of a hat, but half the time the ears come off. Vampire guesses he feeds her too well out of love—she is his darling Bubbles—and that's made her obese, so it's hard to slip Bubbles into the hat before Vampire pulls her out. Her weight slows his sleight-of-hand down. Poet's tried various brands of super glue on Bubbles' ears but the glue is not made to work on rabbit flesh.

So his career as an adult magician has not been doing its best. Adults have to commute to work, balance their checkbooks, and pay utilities—how can they afford to believe in magic? But kids—kids!—they are born to wonder, so Vampire's become a children's magician and works PTA fundraisers, church Sunday schools, and birthday parties. The kids are so thrilled to hold and pet Bubbles they don't care if her ears come off.

Vampire always wears a tuxedo during performances,

to impress, but also because tuxedos have tails that can have hidden pockets. Vampire acquired a dove named Starlight. Vampire loves her too but his assistant, who Vampire lately has been living with, makes Vampire keep Bubbles and Starlight out in the garage. Starlight is always flying out of his tuxedo tails at the wrong time. She is deaf and blind and can't pick up on his cue words or gestures, but to the kids a bird flying out of a man's suit seems good and plenty magic.

The kids also love Vampire's one-legged duck and tailless skunk. These lovely souls he rescued from an animal shelter that ought to be called an animal gas chamber because they don't shelter animals long. The skunk Dottie had been someone's pet and they'd had her fixed so she could no longer spray. Dottie's owners failed to pick her up from the vet after a car ran over her tail. Vampire uses the duck on his guillotine trick. He puts a carrot in a hole above the hole the duck's head sticks through. The carrot gets cut in half by the whooshing silver blade, but the duck comes out, magically, unruffled. The duck loves the trick because she loves to eat chopped carrots. The skunk and Vampire get confused at times during their levitation routine. Dottie the Flying Skunk can levitate six feet up and Vampire passes a hoop over her body to prove there were no hidden wires, but since she's small and black sometimes she'll disappear down his sleeve. Vampire tells the kids to keep quiet so the skunk won't let lose a stink bomb fart that could kill them all with stink. They love the word fart and laugh and laugh. Vampire doesn't tell them Dottie is fixed. Dottie, before her act, sits in an open cage on his magician's table, where the kids can see her. She maintains order because the kids naturally suspect she is fierce.

Vampire met his assistant Cherry at her eighteenth birth-

Chuck Taylor

day and graduation party. Her dad gave her a car and threw a big shindig. Vampire doesn't think the proud father was too happy when Cherry followed him back to his ramshackle house in her new car. "Can I come inside?" She asked, "I can fix your rabbits' years. I work at the mall and have been piercing ears going on three years."

Cherry and Vampire, despite their age difference, have been together two years.

"It's a professional relationship," Cherry says. "I'm not, like, into old guys."

They work four one-hour shows on a Saturday and four on Sunday. At a hundred a show, that's eight hundred a week, or $3,200 a month. Vampire could do more but it's the 1970's and that's good money. He wants to spend much of his time hunting for blood. Vampire remains a lousy magician, but he and Cherry love kids though obviously they have none of their own. When you're lousy you can relax and have a good time. Vampire's stuck to the same tried and true old tricks and never learned new ones. Vampire wouldn't want to leave out any of his animal friends.

Just to let you know, Vampire is not lousy at everything. Vampire's a decent photographer and has had many gallery shows, but photography's a deep dark art as Vampire does it, and nobody buys. Vampire thinks it's the passion behind the art that scares people away, plus most people are not smart enough. This is a democracy, and you're not supposed to say that, so you didn't hear it on this page. The Buddha says to stay disengaged to avoid suffering, and that what's Vampire does, except for his friend Cherry, his magic animals, his crow, and his art photography.

Notice

Vampire's always wondered what's inside you, Cherry. He knows it's more substantial and highflying than the beautiful shape changing, sky-winding clouds, what with your considerable wings. Vampire considered Bing cherries, strawberries, mangoes, pears, and oranges—all the delicious fruits. Although you might not consider it flattering, he's always known you to have a Border collie soul, loving and loyal, and you also have the calm of a small bay on a windless sunny day, and there's a trick to your eyes that can look through the dark stuffed inside the dark to see the light on the other side.

You are also capable of incredible deafness to what you don't wish to hear, as well as unexpected volcano eruptions (especially when drunk). And so Cherry, you have always remained interesting, always contained elements of challenge, of danger that have fascinated Vampire.

Vampire wishes to thank you for sharing these gifts and many more that you probably haven't taken the time to notice that you have. He can't promise to spare your life forever, as you move around and through your world. Hunger is a hard master. But, dear friend, he's going to give it a try.

Chuck Taylor

No Duel

"The reason we can't duel—duel in the way of wily wizards and magnificent magicians—is that the situation is beyond unfair. I am a vampire, yes, no longer invisible in mirrors, no longer afraid of crucifixes or garlic, capable of handling the male or female genders, capable of many divergent shapes human and monster, and yes I do figure widely in the popular imagination, but that does not make me REAL, while you, poet, fuzzy and forgotten, hungry and unpaid, abandoned, left in a corner with your monkey and his cup and rarely read, are nevertheless REAL, and though I have enjoyed at times immense and intense popularity among diverse populations, I am no more than Queen Mab in Mercutio's diatribe in Shakespeare's *Romeo and Juliet*. I'm but a piece of fiction, an emptiness spun from fevered and hysterical imaginations, used primarily by inferior authors for stupid ghoulish effects in order to make a buck.

"Though I, a vampire, in my various forms, inhabit cultures around the world and have deranged men's minds for a thousand years so they commit unspeakable acts— you, you fuzzy dreamer, inhabit all cultures and have lived for at least three thousand years, often called forth and protected by kings and emperors; and from you, poet, from you, off your mere illuminated tongue, come down crashing curses, come blessings penetrating sky and cells, came books that built nations and sacred texts for the faithful to built their cults of gods."

"Vampire, Vampire, what wild and worldly words you spin, and oh how I love to listen. You should consider yourself the first Vampire poet, but look, my friend, I am no more real that you are. I am spun out of words onto this page by the same author who spins you out. We cannot duel because we both are whiffs of the imagination."

"Oh come off it poet. You can do better than that."

"Do you really think I'm real, that I breathe and watch the clouds in a place beyond this page?"

"Stop! Stop! My tongue can't complete with yours. Leave me to the moon, leave me to my nightly flights, but let me have some faith. Let me believe in something. Take it back. Will you, for me? Take it back and leave me with a drop of hope like the drops of blood I nightly seek."

"All right. All right. Have it your way. Believe what you must believe. Believe what you need to believe. Even the author who makes us play this game must have his faith, his illusions, that someone will see these words on the page, be moved and benefited."

"So there is a greater purpose, my Poet man, who speaks for the river of stars?"

"I'd venture to guess so, but don't ask me to try to explain. Your guess, my friend, is as good as mine. I'd guess some aim to things, some purpose, as there are true poets, perhaps, outside this cage of page."

Rats! Yes Rats!

Poet's culture had him trapped, like the infamous rat of oral tales, inside a metal cage, running on a tiny turning metal wheel, day after day after day, week after week after week.

His culture was the rushing clog of Houston traffic. Poet tries to protect his life, and the life of others, by maintaining interval, but when he creates some space to stop, should the car in front of him suddenly stop, cars from other lanes slip in front of him and fill the space to maintain eternal clog. Drivers fight clog but the dog of clog is their omnipotent God.

They need to learn, when stopped still in clog, to burn some incense on the dashboard and say some prayers.

In this Texas city build on gasoline, if you wish to switch lanes and let the drivers behind know your plan, the driver behind in the other lane will speed up so you can't come over into the lane.

Ah so. Poet does the only thing he can, the Houston famous turn-on-your –blinker-as-you-change-lanes dance. No one loves you here. It's all self-interest. They retrain their urge to smash into Poet's shabby truck because it will dent their more expensive status vehicles.

Poet drives the way all others drive in Houston because if he drives any other way he could end up dead—metal crashing, even flaming, dead. He conforms to the dog of clog that is Houston's reigning idol.

That's why Poet once escaped to live in a shabby cabin, thin air high up in the Rocky Mountains way above Boulder, Colorado.

That's why he moved for years across the seas to another nation, to find some other culture that seemed to him a better fit.

Many times Poet's somehow got himself in, or got himself out, of the tiny metal cage of Houston clog. He's a poet and knows no culture can ever be a perfect fit, or keep him in its metal cage forever. Alienation is his stimulating nation.

Poet and Vampire

So long ago Poet loved this vampire because of the Georgia way she talked and the smoky way she smelled, not smiled. He loved her because she could sing and draw and write poems and stories that won awards. He loved her because she was generous and charming. Everybody loved her and everybody was always dropping by the house to visit. She'd gone to some kind of AA for vampires and had been sober, off her addiction to blood, for twenty years—before Poet met her. She didn't even drink the blood of her first husband.

Poet knew their love could never last. The woman was smarter that he was, and faster with the tongue. He knew that in the end she loved her children more that him, and that she would always live with her children, who, along with their drug problems, had been born without vampire genes. Poet can't imagine how she managed to conceive with a human. It boggles the imagination. Some kind of artificial insemination he can guess but never ask. Yet his was a love build on admiration, so rarely could he question what she said or did, but admiration alone can't forever carry love.

Poet began to hate himself for being such a failure. He

had no magical vampire powers. He knew if he were addicted to blood he'd never master the discipline and strength to overcome the need to feed. They often lived apart for six months at a time as they worked separate jobs in different cities.

Eventually she grew distant. She rarely said a word to him, and they didn't even cuddle in bed, which is all they ever did. She was being kind probably, making sure she did not drink his blood and kill him.

Finally he wrote her a letter—they were apart because of jobs again—and she turned down his offer, again, to move where he was. He told her in the next letter that he'd had enough, that thanks to a dream he had the night before, he finally understood that things would never be like they were their first years together.

He couldn't tell her to her face because he feared she'd try to talk him out of it—that she'd argue for another try and knowing she was a vampire he would give in. For a week he got drunk on beer and danced around his small apartment, but eventually the pain grew dull and he began to go out and see others. After a year of misery he slowly began to rediscover happiness. He found a job that paid decent money, and slowly he pulled himself out of the poverty they'd lived in together fourteen years.

He couldn't believe it when he learned, when he left, she was so distraught she could barely move—her, a vampire!—but that faded after not too long. She found herself another one to love, and got happy.

Good Old Stinking Literature

One of the great questions raised by narratives is what to do when you're surrounded, Poet thinks.

You can be surrounded by water (*Robinson Crusoe*), surrounded by white people (*Black Elk Speaks*), surrounded by armies (*War and Peace*), surrounded by mosquitoes and malaria (*Tarzan*), surrounded by zombies, by vampires, otherwise known as critics (*Jack Kerouac*), surrounded by adults (*Rebel without a Cause*), surrounded by enemies with poison gas (*Wilfred Owen*), surrounded by wolves, by rats, perhaps by migrating Monarch butterflies (*Annie Dillard*) or by the fans of Garth Brooks fighting it out with the fans of the Grateful Dead, surrounded by deputized crowds (*Butch Cassidy and the Sundance Kid*), surrounded by saints, by nuns, by surround sound, by fog, by friendly or unfriendly aliens (*Alien & Aliens*), by shmoos (*Lil' Abner*), or by the decadent ultra rich (*The Great Gatsby*).

With such a rich potential for surrounding, stories have struggled to provide escapes, but that's the problem with narratives. They stink and their ends come off as often unconvincing, because stories must end, yet life rumbas or rumbles on. Now that we're back with life, let Poet ask you, HAVE YOU EVER BEEN SURROUNDED? Did a rescuer come? Did you carry a pistol in your pocket or in your purse to fight or bluff your way out? Did you dig a tunnel out and take flight?

Ha! I figured as such, and you never threw yourself in front of a train after a failed love affair (*Anna Karenina*), or poisoned yourself (*Madame Bovary*). Yeah! That's life! It figures a way around like water and does its flowing on.

Never imitate the end of books, Poet says. Mark Twain's classic, *Adventures of Huckleberry Finn*, was "shot to hell," Hemingway said. Ends of books are bad for you—and so may be this one.

Short Tour of El Paso

The albino cat chases the mouse, and Poet sleeps badly, rises early from bed to give the rose of his heart, that little putt-putt, a chance to get warmed up and running.

Poet catches the claptrap bus up Mesa from his Coronado neighborhood—not so trendy neighborhood—caring nothing of Coronado or other slaughtering conquistadors, and gets off at the bakery on the corner across from the plaza downtown.

What will Poet get today to illuminate his tongue? Since he got up he's been dreaming, and it's a secret—not for this poem.

Poet patently waits in line studying the choices in the bakery's glass cases as he has done on and off for forty years. The alligators are long gone from the fountain that William Carlos Williams got off the train and wrote about. Dharma bum Kerouac got off too and walked out of town to sleep in an arroyo. Poet crosses at the light and joins the gems of other old men in the plaza to sit and eat and shine in the brightness. Small children run up and down the walkway between the benches.

During the war, sailors would pick up sailors here in this city of night, Rechy told us. Gilb wrote about young heterosexual love working at the White House Department Store once nearby.

What should Poet write about? The voices in his heart sear up messages in a special Morse Code.

It's About Time for Something Untitled

Poet noticed the black dried chewing gum stuck under the restaurant table when he bent down to pick up the napkin he'd dropped. The icky sight made him think of the black flattened spots of gum on sidewalks. Suddenly his dislike of the human race came out full force. Nothing could be better if the leaders they elected and deserved would send the kids off once again to fight and fail in other impossible wars. We need more Vietnams, Iraqs, Afghanistans, Syrias, and Ukraines. It's what our manufacturers need and stimulates the economy. War's for all to enjoy, except for Poet, of course. He needs to stay behind, demonstrate and publish anti-war writings to prove we've still got democracy.

Poet's convinced he's a good sort of fellow. He has never stuck chewing gum on the underside of a desk or table. He has never spit it out on the sidewalk. He quit chewing when his dentist told him the crap would pull out the fillings in his cavities.

At least on sidewalks the black spots provide jobs for people, good hard minimum wage labor scraping with sharp metal tools and hot water. Poet has seen them slaving on their knees on the sidewalks of the world around McDonald's.

I don't get it. I don't try that hard to be good, Poet

thinks.

Why can't others be good? Lately he's noticed that humans have gotten so indolent they refuse to close the flaps on country mailboxes that the US Post Office made them install so carriers could be lazy and ride around in gas polluting trucks and not walk up to your door.

Maybe it's because Poet's not much interested in status, fame, or money? Maybe it's because Poet spent much of his time doing either nothing or something he loved?

Might he be one of the laughable elect, the chosen?

Peace, Poet, and Vampire

Poet's thinking of anger—the blooming thistle weed in-side his heart, so similar to your anger, dear reader. Po-et's thinking how over time he's learned to wield his an-ger like a hammer and chisel, to cut through the rough hardwood of his days, to make of such material things that are beautiful, bright and curling.

Yes, Poet's thinking of your anger, reader, that in truth is so much like his anger—a dark and waving power. Poet's also thinking how both Vampire and Poet need to water and fertilize their anger in the window box of their bod-ies, to save all that waving beauty—the beauty that tears, the beauty that keeps them going...

Was It Something He Said?

Wherever Poet's lived, on mystic coasts or dull interiors, he's cultivated hiding places, more than one in each location, and for all sorts of situations.

Poet doesn't know who might come—preacher or policeman, constable or Cosa Nostra crook, soldier of the state or of some foreign country. And there are so many species of foreign and domestic spies, full of complicated, twisted lies.

Poet doesn't know when or why they'll come, but since he's the practical peaceful kind and has no wish to fight—and loves so deeply his kingdom of freedom— he'll no doubt take off for one of his hidden overlooked places.

So far, so good, but life is languorous and long.

Poet won't reveal the specifics of where he'll go—only says that he won't go back to his hausfrau home town, that he doesn't take to black holes that have no back doors, and that he'll remain hidden always amongst the multitudes he needs, spreading silently his little sermons on the mount.

One Racist Poem

This will be his first consciously racist poem, but who knows, since Poet is a racist and you're a racist, either consciously or unconsciously, we all probably did something racist in our lives at one time or another.

Right here on this page, Poet is going to tell you how white people and black people cross streets in Central Texas. Is it the same where you live? Observe and decide.

Anyway, when you pull up to a stop sign in your car and stop, black people will cross the street slowly. Poet wants to say they will move like Aunt Jemima's molasses, but that'd be too racist, so Poet won't utter that, yet it seems to him, as a white person, that blacks, when they cross, are putting on a display of both power and trust. The want to make the man wait and wait and wait, and yet they have a faith the man won't get mad and run them over. Well good for these blacks, and the truth is Poet doesn't mind at all. What's the rush? He needs to slow down, hear those lyrics a little clearer on the radio, or make up some new poem lines in his head. A few times he's even smiled and waved, but the pedestrians look straight ahead and don't seem to notice.

Do black people walking do the same molasses walk to black drivers at stop signs? Poet doesn't know. Poet can count on one hand the number of times he's sat next to a black person driving. Three times. That's America for you, but hey, a lot of nations are worse than we are. Take France. Poet's spent time in France and likes the place, but their problems with race are arguably greater than ours—not to say we don't have big problems and a long way to go.

Now if Poet comes to a stop sign and white people are crossing, these folks will hustle along or do a little trot— the polite ones anyway—to show their concern and to not inconvenience you too much with a long wait behind the wheel. After all, a person in a big metal box of a car has got it all over the person walking, raw power-wise. Does poet, when crossing, trust the man behind the wheel? No! That's why he makes a show of trotting.

Now today, Poet was at a stop sign, and a black woman did a little jog across the street so as not block his way long and to get to her bus stop for the ride up to college. She had no real reason to jog because the bus had not come yet. Poet's never seen a black person do that, EVER, and surmised she must have grown up around whites or become friends with a bunch or whites in high school, to pick up that small thing, probably unconsciously.

But as Poet said, he is only "surmising" here. He knows next to nothing about blacks.

What Matters

Poet drove three hundred thirty miles to Shreveport for a cardboard box that wasn't in the corner of the bedroom where he thought he'd left it, it turned out. The box was nothing but a worn old box left behind in a house Poet could no long afford since he'd lost his job.

The box went way back to the packing for the family's move from Villa Park to Evanston, Illinois in 1961. His mother hated the move and refused to assist in the packing. Not long after the move she attempted her first suicide and his parents got quit speaking.

Poet remembers carrying the box upstairs into his first apartment in Evanston. It was full of the books of his childhood, books that gave him strength, books that forgave his weaknesses and taught him how to deal with the slings and arrows of outrageous fortune, books that pointed to all the magic hidden in corners.

Poet's not sure how Poet ended up with the box. How come his sister didn't get it? But the box has been around through many moves for fifty-three years and somehow held together. Poet searched the empty old Shreveport house three times from top to bottom for the stupid box.

He still had to find a job in Austin and heard the job market was good, but could he go on and get by at his ancient age without the box?

Chuck Taylor

The Little Engine that Could Takes a New Tack

In a children's book Poet had a little train, an efficient sweet-hearted machine that always was puffing up and down the black mountains on its tracks, stuttering, "I think I can, I think I can, I know I can, I know I can."

It was the kind of music the railroad company wished to hear, and the engineer wished to hear—a building crescendo of the pressure of stream for the delivery of goods to faraway stations on time—the beef cattle, the beats, the bolts, the wheat, ah, whatever that was heavy and needed over those mountains in distant lands and tongues.

Then one afternoon the little engine jumped onto a sidetrack. It puffed for miles till it reached into the satin dark and stopped to find that the night was made of a million stars put up in patterns by invisible birds whose wings made a magical swooshing.

He heard a gentle singing in the quaking aspens along the railroad tracks. Small birds came out of the woods to eat the seeds that dropped from his grain cars. A bear approached and sniffed his cattle guard.

I can do no more, the little train mused. I must rust here,

if I will rust anywhere, and sing inside the great panorama of this, a quieter life.

Vampire's Gone
Moonbeam

Vampire spends a lot of time outdoors, and has come to know that dust clings to its own life, full of fantastic tales much like his own.

Forget what he's said offhandedly in the past. The dust's not here to figure death and make us miserable. Some comes from cosmic places bearing new messages. It brings a weight that keeps our planet in its place, a counterbalance for the air that spins on off.

Dust knows that its brother soil is singing to the grass, which moves in the wind to fractal rhythms of a higher math.

Take a moment, Vampire would like to tell you. Go out on your front lawn at dusk and sit a while in the cooling summer grass.

We came from dust, and it's all there waiting, how the light is dark, and the dark is light—how it's all interwoven.

Vampire's Death Song

Goodbye all ears and eyes, I wish to swim the deeper seas with the sharks, I want to detect electromagnetism from holes filled with gum beneath my jaw.

Yes goodbye the mundane blue and brown human eyes. Vampire would swim with porpoises with a purpose, to see by sonar clicks through the dark waters into the hidden heart of life. He's had seven hundred years to be with the soil.

Time, you took so many of his children—not biological children but those he loved and the reason for his work and play. Vampire never figured out how there could be glorious beaches if he couldn't shape castles in the bright sunlight along the water, so he let the moonlight take him to other places where he could build castles that glowed of small stone. His almost human form brings him such joy at times that Vampire swims through the air of night almost with the grace of a swallow.

Let Vampire pass over like Christ the explorer. He wants reincarnation, to greet the waters, constant in all places, cold and warm and full of surprising creatures and currents.

Vampire's Ten Proofs for the Existence of God

For Saint Thomas Aquinas

1. The toilets of Los Angeles, New York, Singapore, Tokyo, and London—how they flush and flush without failure.
2. The infinite hairs that have gathered in the hairbrush that he needed to remove all his life—yet still he's got some hair.
3. He's traveled, let's say, to twenty countries, and always good will has shined off faces and his credit card has worked.
4. This father he knew, his daughter held his hand, when he walked her to school, all the way through the fourth grade.
5. When he couldn't make the trip by flying, men he did not know and never saw again stopped in remote desert and helped him get his sad old car out of a deep mud hole.
6. That guy who made the sudden U-turn, as he crossed the street, that guy slammed on his breaks, and his front bumper just kissed his leg.
7. More and more people choose to stay home to interact with their families, who are particles of God, rather than being bored by the outdated rituals and

provincial theologies of mind control churches.

8. Doves, when gathered together in Vampire's neighborhood, become loud on April mornings, and wake him with a hope and trust far grander than the wake up tunes on the radio.

9. Vampire stole a magnet from the hardware store and threw a rock through a neighbor's window. He never got caught, and he never became a criminal.

10. He dials up the divine every night before he falls asleep. The golden sunshine, always there.

Chuck Taylor

Poet Blues

Poet is out of gas. His tires are flat and seats are busted. Poet has been sitting in a farmer's field, at the barbwire fence close to Highway 21, for almost a decade now. His body is rusted and the paint is sun scorched. Poet once had a "For Sale" sign up on the dash, but the letters have faded. Rats have made a nest in the trunk. A copperhead sometimes coils up where the battery used to sit. The back seat, years ago, was a hideaway on summer evenings for two teenage lovers who had nowhere else to go. Poet loved listening to their sweaty whispered secrets. Every once and a while a mockingbird lands on the roof and breaks into song. The varied music makes Poet's engine almost turn over. That's the kind of thing Poet should have wrote, so long ago, he thinks, but was too young to understand.

Vampire, At Last Admitting He Can Write, Tries Again

Today I stood next to the flag draped coffins
Today I read the names of the thousands
Who have died so far in these wars
Noting the cities and states they called home
Looking for my regions, those I may have known.

Today I said in silence my favorite prayer
Today I thought of the paper ribbons
Ubiquitous on the back of pick up trucks
Saying SUPPORT OUR TROOPS.
Today I thought of General De Gaulle

Leader of Free French Forces during World War Two
Leader of the Republic during the Algerian crises,
How he betrayed the hopes of his Generals
And pulled home French troops out of Algeria.
Blood dries fast said the President

Blood dries fast said the great savior of France.
Today I stood next to a flag draped coffins
Today I read the names of the thousands
Saying in silence my favorite prayer.
Blood dries, blood dries

Chuck Taylor

Sing them with pride into the battle
Sing them quiet when they fall
Ship them silent in the flag draped coffins
Slide them back home into the soil
Blood dries, blood dries fast

Finis

Vampire's run the gamut. The gamut has run Vampire, after seven hundred imaginary years. Like the salmon, he's been up his native river to spawn, and knows the final curtain's coming.

Somewhere across the vast universe, lit up like a Christmas tree, a cell is dividing in a place where gravity is not too cumbersome, where the light is lovely and not too blinding.

That cell speaks to all of us. Yes, the cell speaks for all of us. It includes the poets, the pigs, the cows, the crows — and Vampire.

ON THE AUTHOR

Chuck Taylor went to work early, and although it may have inhibited his social skills, the work kept him out of all sorts of trouble, especially as a teenager, innocent and stupid around the ladies. He began mowing lawns and operating a paper route, and then moved on to janitor work and house painting, and later worked as a minor electrician, morgue attendant, lab researcher, cafeteria lineman, dishwasher, daycare worker, part-time records and reference librarian, special collections clerk, bookstore clerk, printer's assistant, furniture mover, children's magician, typist, and soft water salesman. Taylor also worked poets-in-the-schools in Galveston, Beaumont, and Victoria, and as a CETA poet-in-residence for Salt Lake City. As a teacher he has taught at the Universities of Texas at Austin, El Paso, and Tyler, as well as at Austin Community College, Angelo State, and for twenty-five years, Texas A&M in College Station and in Koriyama, Japan. He has been married three times and has three ex-step children, three blood children, and seven grandchildren. Taylor has published two novels, two story collections, two memoirs, and numerous volumes of lined verse and prose poetry. His most recent book, before this new one called *Poet and Vampire*, was *Magical, Fantastical, Alphabetical, Soup* (Pinyon Press). It is not surprising that his first novel, briefly considered for a movie, is called *Drifter's Story*. He feels his path has been one of stable instability.

Praise
for
Chuck Taylor's
Magical, Fantastical, Alphabetical Soup

This book is just what its name implies, a tour through multiplicities of the human heart, a deconstructive exploration of the interpretive mind, a clever philosophical clutch at the divine sweetness of the human soul waiting beneath the exterior.
> —Connie Williams

Chuck Taylor's *Magical, Fantastical, Alphabetical Soup* is the best book of prose I have ever read! It is part philosophy, part flash memoir, and everything prose poetry is supposed to be. Get this book! You won't regret it.
> —Christopher Carmona